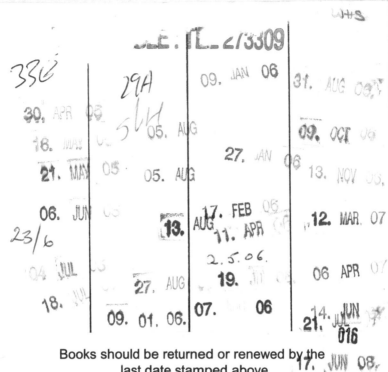

Books should be returned or renewed by the last date stamped above

Awarded for excellence

Kent County Council

THE CAPTAIN'S MESSENGER

When Clare's wealthy, widowed aunt decides to remarry she expects Clare to act as a go-between for herself and Captain Peter Chatham. Peter has no intention of marrying, and to get himself off the hook, introduces the aunt to another officer. While Clare is running messages, a mysterious man who has been attacking women in Bath, kidnaps her. Peter rescues her and realises he might like to marry after all.

ANNE HOLMAN

THE CAPTAIN'S MESSENGER

Complete and Unabridged

LINFORD
Leicester

First published in Great Britain in 2004

First Linford Edition
published 2005

British Library CIP Data

Holman, Anne
    The captain's messenger.—Large print ed.—
Linford romance library
    1. Love stories
    2. Large type books
    I. Title
    823.9'14 [F]

ISBN 1–84395–588–1

Published by
F. A. Thorpe (Publishing)
Anstey, Leicestershire

Set by Words & Graphics Ltd.
Anstey, Leicestershire
Printed and bound in Great Britain by
T. J. International Ltd., Padstow, Cornwall

This book is printed on acid-free paper

1

Early one May morning in 1814, Miss Clare Fountain was enjoying walking along Wood Wells Lane, which was prettily carpeted with bluebells, when she heard female cries. Alerted to assist someone in trouble, Clare left the path and pushed into the undergrowth to investigate.

'Please Sir, let me go!' pleaded a desperate girl's voice.

Horrified to hear a strident male laugh, Clare froze. Her hands prickled with fear as she heard him hiss, 'Shut up girl, or I'll hit you.'

Clare realised a scuffle was taking place behind the bushes ahead. She heard the girl yell again, 'Stop. You're hurting me!'

As the shrieks continued, the man threatened, 'Quieten down, or I will give you something to cry about.'

Clare had always thought this section of the dense woodland possibly dangerous. Thieves — or worse — could lurk in the bushes ready to pounce.

Her fears had now come true. A girl was being attacked and needed help.

But Clare was apprehensive. At twenty-one years old, she was a gentle female. Dare she intervene?

'Help me!'

That anguished cry made Clare angry and overcome her fright. Realising she could well be the victim herself, she first looked around until she saw a short, thick branch. Arming herself, she scrambled deeper into the undergrowth towards the voices.

It didn't surprise Clare to see a wiry officer attired in regimentals pinning a crying maid to a tree trunk by brute force. His distinctive moustache stuck out from either side of his face.

Without hesitation, Clare swept up to the back of the attacker and wielding the branch gave the man's head a forceful thwack.

The fellow leaped away from the girl as blood from the wound trickled down over his eyes, temporarily blinding him as he sank to his knees.

Ignoring his angry curses, Clare grasped the maid's hand and pulled her out of the woods on to the path.

'Oh, thank you, Ma'am,' the girl sobbed, 'I thank you with all my heart!'

'Quickly. We must get away from here before that wretch recovers!' Clare exhorted her to run, and was amazed the girl seemed reluctant to leave the area.

'I can't. I must find my baby.'

Was the girl temporarily crazy after the attack? Clare, anxious to be away before the villain struck again, could have done without any complication. She forced herself to calm down and breath slowly. She asked, 'Where did you leave your child?'

With fearful eyes the maid looked about her and in a voice gasping with panic answered, 'We was coming along this path,' she gulped, 'when that officer came and dragged me away . . . I told him I was a good girl. I didn't want no kissing and such like. But he wouldn't listen, Ma'am . . . he just . . . ' Dissolving into fresh tears the girl seemed too upset to continue.

Still trying to quell her own fears, as the officer might leap out of the woods at any time, Clare had the greatest difficulty resisting the temptation to run off. But a child was mentioned and she must make sure the infant was safe.

Fortunately, apart from being upset, the girl didn't looked harmed. Noticing the girl's clean pinafore — although her cap was askew — Clare enquired, 'Are you a nursemaid?'

Sobbing, she replied, 'Yes, Ma'am. I'm Lady Brocklehurst's nursemaid.'

Clare had heard nothing but good of young Lord and Lady Brocklehurst. They had a baby son, William, so this was obviously the child the nursemaid was talking about.

'Was the child in a perambulator?'

The maid took out her handkerchief,

wiped her eyes and blew her nose. This operation seemed to bring her back to her senses. 'Yes, Billy was in his pram. It must be near here. Don't let that brute get the baby, please.'

Clare thought quickly, if I went one way and the nursemaid the other, we would spot the child's perambulator easily. But the nursemaid seemed in no state to be left alone.

'I think we should walk together first this way,' she said pointing ahead, 'and if we don't see Billy we can turn and go the other way.'

'You are very kind, Ma'am.'

As they walked towards the village of Clifton on the Hill, Clare said, 'Don't call me Ma'am. I'm a servant like you.'

'You don't sound like one, Miss.'

Clare breathed heavily. 'I wasn't brought up a working girl. But I am now. although my position as companion to Lady Hadfield is more tedious than hard work.'

The nursemaid's wet, lashed eyes looked at her wide-eyed. 'Are you companion to Lady Hadfield, the widowed heiress?'

'I am.'

'Cor! That must be a comfortable billet. In that great house.'

Clare smiled at the little nursemaid. Like herself, the girl possessed a healthy complexion, a ready smile and lively, caring spirit. 'Indeed it is.'

To their relief, the baby carriage was round the corner. Without the brake on, it had rolled into the wood a little way but inside, the sleeping baby had no notion of the danger his nursemaid had been in during the past fifteen minutes.

Clare held the nursemaid's arm to prevent her from picking up the child in her joy of finding him safe. 'Don't waken him,' she said smiling at the little boy's peaceful, slumbering face. 'He won't know anything about the attack and shouldn't be disturbed. Now show me where you live and I'll go home with you.'

The nursemaid was most grateful and soon seemed to forget her ordeal as she pushed the pram towards Clifton, saying her name was Annie Willis, that she liked working for the Brocklehursts, and would never come this way again. Although she liked to walk by the river as you got a lovely view of the Avon and Hotwells, whatever the time of the year. And young Billy liked to see the ships on the way to, and out of, Bristol docks. 'and he loves the ducks that nest alongside the river marshes, too.'

Clare sighed. 'It will be a shame if you let that unfortunate incident prevent you from coming this way again.'

'Yes, it will, Ma'am. But I daren't go that way again now.'

'Please don't keep calling me Ma'am.'

'What shall I call you then?'

'Clare. Miss Clare Fountain is my name. Lady Hadfield is my aunt.'

The maid's eyes widened. 'You're related to Lady Hadfield? There!' exclaimed Annie. 'I thought you was a lady. Niece to Lady Hadfield. How about that!'

Clare laughed. 'A poor niece of Lady

Hadfield, remember. Her Ladyship has taken me in like a stray kitten.'

Annie giggled and Clare was pleased the nursemaid was getting over her ordeal. 'Is Lady Hadfield nice to you? I've heard she's a bit, well . . . odd.'

Now it was Clare who giggled. 'Yes, Annie, she is reclusive.' Clare didn't explain that her aunt was lazy too. She added, 'But she's kind,' which she was.

The baby awoke stretching and gurgling. Billy's big blue eyes gazed at Clare. Then he struggled, waving his little hands in the air until Annie sat him up. He beamed, and babbled happily in baby language, until they arrived at Lord and Lady Brocklehurst's fine house and had to part company.

Clare suggested, 'I usually take a walk before Lady Hadfield gets up in the morning. So unless she is unwell . . . ' as she sometimes was from over-indulging in food or wine the previous evening, but Clare didn't elaborate on that, 'I could meet you at

8

say, eight o'clock, in the mornings if it is fine. We could walk through the woods together, stroll along the river-bank for a while and then come back. You would be quite safe with me. That vile officer wouldn't dare tackle two of us together. For I'm sure men who attack women are cowards at heart.' If they had a heart, which Clare doubted.

'Oh, thank you,' Annie cried, 'I'd like that.'

Clare smiled back at the nursemaid, relieved to see she thought this plan a good idea and wouldn't have to worry about taking the baby out for a walk next day.

'I'll meet you here at eight tomorrow then,' Clare said, waving goodbye, 'and I'll bring some bread for Billy to feed the ducks.'

'Thank you. He'd love that.'

Walking away, Clare had to return again towards Bristol as she had been out that morning because she had a message to deliver. Not a task she relished, but she frequently had to grin and bear it when her aunt demanded she did this and that, which was not to her liking.

Yesterday she'd been told to write a letter to Captain Peter Chatham, which shouldn't have been an arduous task. But the letter had been embarrassing to write because of the nature of the private correspondence.

Clare's face had become scarlet when she was told that Aunt Maud was bored with widowhood and missed the intimate idea of marriage. That at the age of thirty, her aunt had decided to marry again. Hearing Peter Chatham, who she'd known as a boy, was back home after serving in the navy, retired injured after the Battle of Trafalgar, she'd decided he would be her quarry.

Aunt Maud had been previously successful in entrapping one of the richest, oldest, titled husbands in the district, so that when he died after a few years of marriage, she'd become an exceedingly rich widow. So now her aunt believed she would be able to catch another husband without too much trouble. And as she was too lazy to write her own correspondence, she'd asked her paid companion to write the missive.

What Clare now carried in her reticule — or had she put it in her pocket? — was a note composed by herself, requesting Captain Chatham to call upon Lady Hatfield to discuss marriage, which Clare considered to be a saucy request and certainly an indiscreet thing to ask of any gentleman. But, not wishing to disobey and annoy her aunt — and possibly lose her livelihood — Clare had dutifully penned the missive.

★   ★   ★

Now, after waiting until a baker's lad came along so that she could walk down Wood Wells Lane again with him, she stopped to bid him goodbye. Then she checked and discovered she couldn't find the letter anywhere. It had gone — she'd lost it!

Obviously during the time she was rescuing Annie in the woods, the letter had fallen out of her pocket. Dear me. Clare just hoped whoever found it would give it to Captain Chatham as his name was on the envelope.

But as she stood there perplexed, who should come limping along but the tall, stern, but good-looking gentleman himself! She recognised Captain Peter Chatham, ship-shape in a dark blue coat and buff trousers, and using a walking stick.

He lived in comfortable retirement in a fine house overlooking Lower Green, on the south-west side of Bristol, well situated for using the spa waters to aid his recovery. And daily walks were helping him to improve the use of his legs.

Clare had hoped to deliver the letter without having to meet the gentleman her aunt was determined to entrap with the impassioned sentiments she'd been forced to write. Now she felt she wanted to disappear down a nearby coal hole. But there was no escape. On one side of the street were three-storied houses and on the other a steep cliff down to the River Avon.

Peter Chatham's keen seaman's eyes spotted Clare long before she saw him. He'd already recognised her as Lady Hadfield's companion, and was faintly amused to see her wanting to turn tail and run, when there was nowhere to go unless she fancied an early morning dip in the river.

He was curious to know why the young lady was in such a dither on seeing him. When he'd met her before she'd always seemed genteel and composed, as a companion should be, although her bright blue eyes struck him as intelligent.

Known to have been a strict, but fair-minded naval officer to his sailors, he wondered if his painful injuries had added, not only grey to his hair, but had also formed disagreeable lines on his face? Or maybe living alone, as he did now, his monk-like existence had given him a forbidding presence, which frightened young women?

'Good morning to you,' he called out as cheerily as he could manage. He was gratified when Clare — who he thought was exceedingly attractive — smiled back at him. On the few occasions when he'd met Miss Clare, he'd decided she was far too charming to be saddled as Lady Hadfield's companion.

Not that he disliked Maud, but she was self-centred and dull. And the Captain was well aware she was angling for a new husband — and he was definitely not the man for her.

Now, seeing she could not avoid him, Miss Clare came up to him and returned his bow. Although her rosy cheeks glistened as though she was a little embarrassed as she said, 'Good morning, Captain Chatham. I was coming towards your house because I've a letter for you from Lady Hadfield.'

Her voice lowered and sounded

disappointed, 'But, I'm sorry, sir. I seem to have lost it on the way.'

Peter's lips raised slightly. So that was why she was embarrassed. He wasn't concerned about a message from Maud Hadfield going astray. It was probably only an invitation for dinner.

Seeing he was not dismayed to find his letter missing, the girl suggested, 'I'll go back and look for it.'

As he could detect she didn't seem to relish a search for the letter, he promptly offered to accompany her and much to his amazement she readily agreed.

Now, he thought, that is most surprising. This young lady does not seem to mind my austere company after all. She seems quite happy to walk with me. This discovery made him happy.

He didn't know of course that Clare was reluctant to return to the woods in case the officer was there who'd attacked Annie. But he soon learned about it as they walked along and Clare told him.

15

Clare's father had been a naval captain, killed at the Battle of the Nile, so she was used to sailors and had no difficulty talking to them.

Peter, who'd been listening intently cleared his throat. 'You say the attacker wore a uniform. Can you describe it to me?'

Clare pursed her lips as she pondered. 'Well,' she said at last, 'I only saw him for a short while. I recollect he wore a red army coat and white breeches. And he had silver lace trims, that's how I knew he was an officer.'

'Was there a colour on the facings of his jacket or on his sleeve cuffs? And had he epaulettes on his shoulders? That would tell me his regiment.'

Clare shook her head. 'It's no use you asking me, sir. I don't remember any details. It all happened so quickly. I was concerned with getting the maid away from him.'

Captain Chatham's deep voice went down to its lowest, 'Quite so.'

They walked on for a bit. Suddenly

he asked, 'Did you notice his shako plate?'

'Shako?'

'I mean his hat. Had it a cockade or a plume?'

'Ah, yes. His black stove pipe hat had fallen off. But I'm afraid I didn't notice if it had any pattern on it.' Clare then added, 'But he had a distinctive walrus moustache.'

Peter didn't reply. As he scratched his eyebrow he was trying to think who the attacker could be. He knew most of the gentry in the area. Many army officers were on half-pay, and many had recently been dismissed from the army because there was no war going on as Napoleon was safely imprisoned on the island of Elbe.

Most military men — if not clever — were right thinking and would not attack a maid. But there were always some disreputable men amongst their ranks. He'd known a few. Unfortunately, from the description this young lady had given him, it sounded as if the villain might be Colonel Rupert Rufus, because that gentleman had a distinctive moustache.

Which was a pity if it were so, as Colonel Rufus in his opinion, was not a bad fellow. He'd been decorated for bravery. But that didn't mean he'd not now become a cowardly seducer of young women. Peter decided he would have to investigate the matter. Unpleasant though it would be, he would have to challenge his old acquaintance.

It was not his way to prevaricate. He would pay Colonel Rufus a visit as soon as he possibly could. If indeed Rupert Rufus was attacking women, then someone should put a stop to it immediately.

2

Clare was aware she was alone with a gentleman and entering the woods again, which was not considered proper for a lady. But she didn't feel afraid of being with Captain Chatham. The Captain seemed like a man who would protect her from harm so she felt safe with him.

It wasn't difficult for them to find the spot where Annie had been attacked. Nor did they have difficulty in spotting the Captain's letter, which was on the ground, and to Clare's mortification, somewhat crumpled.

'Well, I'll leave you now,' said Clare, keen to get away before he read it.

'No,' he declared forcefully, 'after what happened earlier, you will not go without me to escort you home.' The Captain was used to giving crisp commands. Then hooking his walking stick on a handy tree branch and leaning against the oak, he opened the letter, and to her dismay began reading it.

Hot with embarrassment, Clare looked down on the ground.

There, amongst the dry leaves and twigs on the earth she saw something glitter. It was a silver button. Bending down she saw it was a military button, one that had probably fallen off the attacker's coat when he'd been struggling with Annie. Clare clenched the button in her hand then popped it in her pocket.

Hearing her companion muttering, 'Hmm!' she looked up and saw to her relief he had a smile on his lips. He was scratching his eyebrow with this thumb as if trying to think how to react to the impertinent epistle.

'Well now,' he said, 'I need to reply to this dispatch.'

He looked down at her but she hadn't the courage to look back at him and turned away pretending to admire the woodland bluebells.

He cleared his throat. 'You may tell your aunt, Lady Hadfield, that I shall be giving her request my closest consideration. Yes, tell her I will call tomorrow as I have another important call to make today.'

With his message firmly in her mind, Clare gave a curtsey. 'Very well, sir, I will tell her. Now I must get back or my aunt will wonder where I am.'

'Quite so.'

He stretched out to grasp his stick and indicated they were to walk back together towards Clifton.

'So you act as secretary to your aunt, do you, Miss Fountain?' he asked suddenly.

Clare started. 'Why yes, I do many things for her.'

'Hmm.'

Clare felt uncomfortable. She had the strong feeling he was no idiot and had already decided her aunt could not have composed and written such a well-written letter.

Clare now wished she'd had the

sense to make a few spelling mistakes when writing it, as she was sure her aunt was not as careful as she was. And she wished she'd not changed what her aunt had told her to write, which was far more forthright than Clare had put down.

On top of that, she'd made the error of allowing her aunt to sign the letter, and it must be obvious to this sharp naval officer that the handwriting on the letter and the signature were not in the same hand.

Oh dear me, how distressing it was to think he'd guessed who'd written the letter!

The only good thing was he didn't seem in the least upset. He seemed amused, but his amusement annoyed Care intensely. She was stuck in the middle and she didn't know what to say. How could she explain that if she'd refused to write the letter she might be in the poorhouse by now?

But it was no use crying over spilled milk, what was done was done, Clare decided. The Captain may have fathomed that she had written those words of passion, but given the chance, she would make it clear that they were words dictated to her.

She had to behave as coolly and discreetly as a paid assistant should. And if Aunt Maud did succeed in winning the Captain over, and he married her, then Clare would hope she would be permitted to continue in her post. So she must continue to act as an impassive messenger and not allow her feelings on the matter to get in the way.

The Captain, who had also been thinking as they walked along in companionable silence, had come to a decision too. He said, 'Now before you go, Miss Fountain, I suggest that if you have any more messages for me that you do not come this way alone. At least, not until this unsavoury character who waylays young ladies has been sent off to a penal colony in Australia. Walk along Cow Lane or College Street where there are houses.'

Clare looked at him and noted he seemed serious as if he did care for her safety.

The Captain, after admiring her bluebell-coloured eyes said, 'I can't see that Lady Hadfield will give in easily, can you? Even if I tell her I never intend to marry.'

Hit by his comment she frowned. 'Sir?'

'Oh, I think you know what I mean,' he said with a little smile on his lips. 'I think you are well aware that your aunt has her claws out for me. She will continue to try and persuade me to marry her if she lives to be a hundred!'

Clare giggled. It was no use pretending she didn't know what her aunt was like. 'Yes, indeed. I fear you might be right!'

There, now she had admitted she knew what was in the letter! But she was relieved the Captain was taking it all in good humour. His eyes met hers and they enjoyed the joke together.

'So,' he said as they approached the

long driveway up to Knowle Park where Lady Hadfield lived, 'I suggest when you have another message from her to deliver, you come to the Hotwells coffee room where I shall be found in the morning at eleven o'clock.'

He took out his watch from his fob waistcoat pocket and examined it in naval style as if he were missing the sound of a ship's bell, which regulated the lives of seamen. Clare thought he must be an exacting time-keeper, and she must bear that in mind when dealing with him. He would be at the coffee room promptly at eleven. If she came much before or after the hour, she might miss seeing him.

To her surprise, Clare found she was almost sorry to have to bid him goodbye, and was pleased to think any further communication between them would take place at a delightful venue as a coffee room in the Spa.

Clare had felt for some time that being her aunt's companion kept her away from society. Having the chance to go to a venue where the fashionably-dressed people met and gossiped was going to be a treat.

'Why, that is a splendid idea,' exclaimed Clare. 'But how will you know which days I will bring a message for you?'

'Young lady, I go to Hotwells every day for treatment. Then I take a drink in the coffee room before I walk home for lunch.'

'I see,' thinking his life was no more exciting than hers. But then he had been a sailor and seen a great deal of the world. And fought with Admiral Nelson. Maybe he felt his days for adventure were over.

As he bowed and said good day, he remarked, 'Oh, and don't bother to write next time. Just give me the main message, like a signal. A dispatch by word of mouth will suffice.'

He swung round and hobbled off before Clare could reply.

She had to smile as she watched his figure disappearing down the hill. He had shown himself to be a man she could like. No wonder her aunt wanted to marry him!

But the Captain said he wasn't a marrying man. Now why that should niggle Miss Clare Fountain she just didn't know.

She almost skipped up the drive with a lift on her lips and had to adjust her bonnet and compose herself before she let herself into the big house by the side door the servants normally used.

★   ★   ★

After dinner that evening Clare felt she could not confide in her aunt about the attack made on the nursemaid, because Maud would not consider this a proper subject to discuss. Nor could Clare admit she was a little scared to go out alone now in case she was attacked. But she knew servants — and she was considered one — had to fend for themselves. So she would just have to be careful if she went out.

Instead she had to listen to her aunt's chatter.

Maud was reclining like a large seal on her chaise-longue in her drawing-room as Clare came up to her with her after-dinner coffee. 'Black bombazine and crape. I'm heartily sick of wearing those dreary clothes. Edwin's been dead for months and I'm still expected to mourn. What kind of impression will I make on Peter Chatham when he comes, while I'm attired like a witch?'

Clare placed the coffee cup on the elegant little side-table near her aunt and replied, 'Well, you are now beyond the time you should wear full mourning. Couldn't you wear half mourning? Select some quiet colours such as white, lilac or brown to wear. Adorn your gowns with some black ribbons.'

Her aunt's plump, prettier face when younger, smiled at her. 'I haven't any of those colours in my stock of clothes. I like bright colours.'

Clare smiled, 'You could get some new gowns.'

'Why yes, I could,' Maud said, livening up. 'The weather is fine at last, so some new clothes would raise my spirits. And you could do with some new clothes too. I don't want to be seen in public with a dowdy companion, do I?'

Clare's eyes gleamed. Having some new clothes would be wonderful. Since her parents died and she'd come to live at Knowle Park she'd been unable to replenish her clothes, and although she'd patched and mended them she could do no more to prevent herself from looking like a rag-bag.

Seeing her niece looking pleased with her suggestion, Maud began to talk aloud to herself about the new clothes she would order from the dressmaker and the bonnets and gloves she would need.

No more mention was made of Clare's wardrobe and Clare hoped she'd not forget. Yet, she began to fantasise on what she would like to have, just in case her aunt mentioned the matter again.

Maud's mind then went on to the visit Captain Peter Chatham intended to make the following day.

'I must make a favourable impression. There's no time to shop or acquire a new gown before then. In some ways I wished he'd waited a week before coming so that I could have acquired a new one. It's so important to get every detail right, Clare. If you wish to trap a man, that is.'

Clare's mouth quivered. She didn't think the Captain would be entrapped by a woman's wardrobe! Although being a Navy man he wouldn't approve of disorderly dress either, ragged and mended gowns like hers.

'He may offer to take me to a musical evening or to the assembly rooms. What do you think of that, Clare? Have you been taught to dance?'

'Alas, no, Ma'am.'

'Then you are to take dancing lessons. I don't suppose I'll be able to dance more than once with Captain

Chatham. I used to enjoy dancing but I find dances these days are so energetic and I tire easily. So he will need a dance partner.'

'But Ma'am, he's lame.'

'Not for much longer. He told me last time I met him he will be walking normally very soon.'

Clare was pleased to hear that. 'But as I can't dance, what shall be done?'

Maud looked her up and down. 'You will have to take lessons immediately of course. Arrange to go tomorrow.'

'But lessons cost money!'

'My dear Clare. Have the Dancing Academy bill sent to me. And have your clothes bill sent to me. You must have some decent ball gowns, kid gloves and slippers to wear if you are to dance with the Captain.'

Knowing her aunt had plenty of money, Clare didn't argue. She felt thrilled. From being an outcast from society she was to have some new clothes, and was to attend balls and assemblies. It seemed too exciting to be true.

The conversation ended by Aunt Maud telling Clare, 'I suppose I'll have to make the effort to go shopping. But I'll expect you to trot down the town, frequently, and get most of the things I want.'

'Yes, Aunt,' Clare agreed with sparkling eyes convinced those shopping trips would be a pleasure rather than an arduous duty.

★ ★ ★

Meanwhile, Captain Peter Chatham was visiting Colonel Rupert Rufus.

The Colonel's shabby lodging house was a poor reflection of his previous status as a high-ranking officer of His Majesty's army. Indeed Peter felt quite sorry that a man of his calibre should be reduced to such a sorry half-pay living.

But that was no excuse for him to attack young women.

As an ex-military man himself, and having had to deal with bawdy lower deck behaviour, Peter had no qualms about being refined or prudish in accosting the Colonel with the matter.

'Colonel Rufus, it is clear to me you are not able to afford a wife or even a mistress. Have you taken to attacking hapless women?'

'Captain Chatham,' protested the Colonel whose face was almost as red as his coat, 'I do not force myself on women. Never have. Never will.'

'The attacker was described as a man like you. Your moustache in particular is most outstanding. No-one I know of has whiskers like yours.'

The Colonel fingered his long sweeping moustache. 'I suppose that is true. But there are always newcomers arriving at the Spa. When did you say this attack took place?'

'Early this morning, sir.'

The Colonel gave a grunt. 'Do I understand this witness is prepared to swear it was I who committed this crime? I don't know what can be done against such damning evidence. Once women start gossiping . . . I might as well shoot myself.'

The Captain observed the crestfallen man. His past bravery in battle was forgotten. His rank gave him no standing because of his empty pockets. Now he was being accused of being dishonourable.

Peter didn't like crushing him further. Indeed he couldn't see any evidence of him being struck on the head as Miss Fountain said had happened.

Suddenly Peter felt the man was innocent of any wrong-doing. The Colonel needed support. 'Colonel Rufus,' he said, 'I came here to inform you of what I was told about the incident. I believe the witness was telling the truth — but she may be mistaken in her description of the attacker. I have no intention of spreading rumours, only of stopping the villain. I should like to help you.'

The Colonel's eyes watered and he used his fingers to wipe them. Peter suspected he didn't possess a handkerchief. 'I appreciate your offer, Captain. You're a good fellow.'

Peter went over and clapped the man on his shoulder. 'Now don't despair, sir. There are several things that can be done. First, tell me, where were you early this morning?'

The Colonel's eyes looked hopeful. 'Here. I was in bed all this morning. Can't afford breakfast. Can't afford to eat more than one meal a day.'

Peter looked around this cold attic room and saw no sign of comfort or food. But it was orderly and clean. He asked, 'Can anyone prove you were here?'

'I don't know. I suppose one or two of the other tenants may be able to say I didn't leave the house this morning.'

'Well, we shall hope so.'

Peter felt more convinced the Colonel was not the culprit. He paced the floor deciding what could be done.

Then an idea flashed into his mind. 'Now Colonel,' he said, 'I suggest we wander around the tavern and take an early lunch — at my expense of course — because I have thought of a good way out of your predicament.'

The Colonel's eyes blinked fast.

Peter was pleased to see the Colonel looking as if he still had some fight left in him. So he said encouragingly, 'Come sir, find your hat. Let me brush your jacket. There, now put your chin up and shoulders back. Show the world you are no skulking rogue. Come, we will seek the villain together.'

The Captain eyed the Colonel up and down and decided he was still a man with reasonable good looks and presence. Nor was he a fool. Indeed, although the Colonel was down-at-heel, he was still an eligible gentleman.

'Colonel Rufus,' explained Peter as they walked to the tavern, 'I have a plan to introduce you to a lady who is looking for a gentleman to wed. She has her eyes on me, but I have no wish to get married. I'm content to remain a bachelor. But if you can charm her . . . and you marry her, you'll be well set up, because she is very wealthy.'

'Ah! God bless you, sir,' said the Colonel, grateful to see an escape route from his problems.

3

The following day, a gig sped up the drive to Knowle Park House. Captain Peter Chatham got out of it, without the help of a walking stick, and rapped on the front door. He looked beautifully turned out in his naval uniform of best blue cloth with fine lace at his neck, white breeches and silk stockings. Clare, who happened to be at an open upstairs window, almost fell out of it looking down at him.

'He has certainly come a' courting,' she muttered to herself as she raced downstairs to open the front door and let him in before the butler appeared.

'I feel I should be able to pipe you aboard,' she quipped as she gave him a smile and a curtsey.

He removed his three-cornered hat and bowed. 'There's no need to set everyone's teeth on edge with that shrill greeting,' he replied, 'I much prefer your sunny smile anyway.'

She blushed at the compliment. 'I see you are not using your stick today.'

'I thought I'd better stand on my own two legs on this occasion.'

Clare looked at him admiring his determination to present himself to her aunt as a fit man although she feared he might be in pain.

Seeming to understand her concern for him he entered the house saying, 'I was hit and pinned down by the rigging and part of a mast at the Battle of Trafalgar. The sailors had to peel me off the deck.'

Amazed he told her so candidly about his condition, Clare felt he now regarded her as a friend.

'I'm truly sorry to hear that, sir.'

'Don't be. I am like a ship in dry dock being refitted out. I'll be as good a new very soon.'

'That is good to hear,' she said in all sincerity and looked up into his eyes. His face showed lines of suffering but his eyes were as clear as deep sea pools, and she wanted to stand looking at them forever.

'Lady Hadfield is expecting you,' Clare said, coming to her senses. 'She is upstairs in her drawing-room awaiting your arrival.'

'Show me up then,' the Captain said, stretching to his full height and looking severe again.

The butler who'd appeared in the hall, turned away as he saw the visitor climbing the grand staircase with her Ladyship's companion.

'Before you leave me,' the Captain said quietly, 'I want to tell you that I went to see an army officer who fitted your description of the man who attacked the nursemaid.'

'Oh yes?'

'I am convinced it was not Colonel Rufus. Although he wears a red army coat and has a fine moustache.'

'What made you decide he was not the rogue?'

The Captain put his finger to his

mouth because they were nearing the drawing-room. 'He had no sign of being hit on the head,' he explained in a hushed voice. 'And his landlady told me he'd not been out that morning.'

Clare bent her head near his to answer in a whisper, 'What can be done about the matter now?' She liked being so close to him she could admire his personal cleanliness and the fresh smell of his after-shave cologne.

The Captain whispered back. 'Say nothing of this affair to anyone. It must not reach Society's tittle-tattlers. And tell the nursemaid not to gossip — although I know she might well have told the Brocklehurst servants already.

'I will look out for other officers who might be the villain. Can you meet me at eleven in the Spa coffee room tomorrow? I will tell you of any development in solving the crime.'

Clare felt a thrill of excitement at being considered a partner in his investigation. 'Yes, sir,' she agreed readily.

'And don't go down Wood Wells Lane alone.'

His command was curt, but Clare knew him well enough now to know he only meant to give her a strong warning for her own safety.

★ ★ ★

Clare and the Captain had reached the drawing-room double doors. Clare knocked, and having announced the Captain, she closed the doors after he strode in.

'Lady Hadfield, how well you look,' the Captain exclaimed after he'd bowed.

'And you are recovered I see, Captain Chatham,' Maud replied from her chaise-longue, as she hadn't moved quickly enough to rise.

'Not quite. I have a way to go before I'm entirely hale and hearty.'

He came forward, kissed her hand, and sat on a Hepplewhite chair near her.

'But,' he continued, 'I'm working at

it. I take treatment at the Spa daily and go for long walks. Up and down Brandon Hill I find is excellent exercise. I enjoy walking in the countryside. Do you?'

'I, er, well I don't go out often,' Maud looked at his lean frame sceptically.

'So you will not share my enthusiasm for walking three or four miles daily?'

Aghast at the suggestion, Maud's hands fluttered in the air, 'Of course I don't walk. I use my carriage.'

Peter paused. Then he suggested, 'Perhaps you prefer dancing?'

Maud looked like a startled hen. 'I can enjoy a dance or two. And if you care for more than that, I've instructed my niece, Clare, to take dancing lessons so that she can dance with you.'

'Splendid.' Peter smiled, although the only dance he knew was the hornpipe he learned when he was a midshipman. He made a mental note that he must take some dancing lessons, too.

Maud, who had prepared herself for

this encounter, found the reason for his coming was being ignored. He was talking about exercise, which she was not keen on. So she asked bluntly, 'Did you receive my proposal?'

'Indeed I did.'

Maud looked at his impassive expression. 'Well?'

Peter gave a cough. 'Well, Ma'am, I have to decline the honour of marrying you. I have sworn to remain a single gentleman.'

Maud looked crestfallen. 'Why? I want to marry again.'

'I know you do. That is why I have a gentleman lined up to meet you.'

Maud put her chubby face on one side asking, 'How do you know he is suitable for me?'

Peter cleared his throat. 'That will be for you to decide. But I must warn you that there is a secret scandal surrounding him at present.'

Maud looked interested. 'What kind of a secret scandal?'

'It is something he has been accused

of, which I do not believe he did.'

'How intriguing. Do tell me more.'

'Only if you promise to keep the information to yourself. Don't go gossiping about it to anyone.'

Maud was sitting up alert to what he had to say. 'I don't gibble-gabble. In fact I don't see anyone very much.'

'Ah,' exclaimed Peter, thinking how sad it was such a young lady should be wasting her life away on a chaise-longue.

Maud looked curious. 'Does he gamble? Drink? Or has he lost his marbles?'

Peter smiled. 'I believe he plays cards, and drinks in moderation. And he strikes me as being reasonably intelligent. He is certainly brave. He was decorated in Spain by Wellington.'

'An army officer, is he? I don't mind that, provided he doesn't expect me to go tramping around the countryside with him. But why hasn't he married? There are many widows wanting husbands and Misses wanting partners at the Spa.'

'Well, I understand the gentleman has no means whatsoever. He is as poor as a church mouse.'

'I see. So he is looking for a rich wife?'

Peter smiled at her. 'I don't doubt he would prefer a rich one to a penniless one. However, it is for you to decide if you would like to meet him. I can only say that I find him honourable. I think you might deal well together, which would suit you both I believe. Do you wish me to arrange for him to call?'

Fascinated by the expression of uncertainty on Maud's face, Peter waited for her decision.

One trait Maud had, which she used to excess on herself, was that she was indulgent. She was a forgiving person. She was the kind of woman who could overlook others' faults. And provided the gentleman who was seeking a wife was able to tolerate her indulgences, then she decided she was prepared to overlook his. Quite how he'd become so penny-pinched was due to carelessness, she decided.

If she married him she would allow him a generous allowance and not permit him to be totally in control of her fortune. She was sure a lawyer could arrange that.

Any scandal she heard about him, Peter had assured her, could be ignored. Because she trusted Peter's word that the scandal was unjustified.

'Well, I don't suppose it will do any harm to meet him,' she said, pretending not to be as interested as she was.

Peter nodded. 'Indeed, you can go out for a drive together if you wish. And see him at the assembly rooms. Several meetings will help you to decide if you like him and wish to continue a friendship.'

'Who is he? Do I know him?'

'His name is Colonel Rupert Rufus.'

Maud shook her head, no bell sounded in her head, she hadn't heard of him. But the suggestion of meeting an unknown eligible gentleman had brightened the lady's eyes, and Peter had no doubt that if she liked Rupert, then he would have little chance of escaping from her bridal bower. Which might well suit them both.

'Well,' he said, standing and bowing, 'if you are in agreement I will inform the gentleman that you are willing to meet him.'

Maud made the effort to rise from her reclining chair and returned his bow. 'Yes,' she said, 'you may invite him here for me to inspect him.'

'Very good.' Peter walked to the door then turned to see Maud had already sank down on her couch again. 'And may I use your companion, Miss Fountain, as a messenger with his reply?'

Maud nodded dreamily. She seemed already to be thinking of her next conquest and anxious to be rid of her visitor.

He grinned, amazed he'd achieved what he wanted so easily. 'And may I use her for messages for further arrangements, when required?'

'Why, of course, Captain Chatham.

My companion, Clare, is a discreet girl. I don't think we need fear she might blab about this matter to anyone. Let her run messages for you by all means. Good day, Captain, and thank you.'

Leaving Maud lying with her hand on her beating heart thinking about a new suitor, enabled Peter to leave her Ladyship without upsetting her. He breathed a sigh of relief after he'd bid her goodbye, thinking he'd got himself off the hook and was able to continue his bachelor existence contentedly.

He always felt more comfortable in men's company yet he couldn't help hoping he'd see Clare again before he left.

So he was pleased to hear her playing softly on the pianoforte. It was an enchanting melody and she made a charming sight, he thought, looking at the back of her neat figure and admiring her swept-up hair adorned with ribbons that fell about her slender neck.

Although the door was open he knocked on the music room door. She stopped playing immediately and stood up by the piano stool, 'Did you find things went well, sir?' she enquired with a little curtsey.

He smiled as he bowed. 'It was a victory.' Coming into the grand room he came near her and said quietly, 'I have persuaded your aunt to abandon me as a suitor.'

Knowing her aunt would not suit him, Clare felt pleased about that. 'Is she upset?'

'Not at all. I have given her another lead.'

'I hope you are not leading her astray, Captain? My aunt may be indolent but I wouldn't wish any harm to come to her — '

'Neither would I, I assure you, Miss Fountain.'

Clare smiled at him, which quite took his breath away. Indeed he found it difficult to concentrate on what he wanted to tell her as he found everything about her enchanting. Those pearly teeth and dewy lips of hers made him want to kiss her.

How extraordinary he should think of kissing Miss Fountain!

He cleared his throat. 'Hum. Well now. I will expect you to be at the coffee room at eleven tomorrow, shall I? I hope to have a favourable message for you to deliver to your aunt.'

'Yes, I will be there,' Clare replied, wondering who the gentleman the Captain had found for his aunt could be. The gentleman would need to be a very exceptional character to move Aunt Maud, thought Clare.

Before he left the captain reminded her again to avoid going along Wood Wells Lane alone.

For the rest of that day, Clare's previous interests of reading, tinkering on the piano and cutting flowers in the garden to decorate the house, were curtailed. She found herself engaged, not only as the Captain's messenger, but also planning to acquire new clothes for her aunt, and herself.

'Trot into Bristol this afternoon and

get me some fashion plates from the dressmaker's,' Aunt Maud said. 'And take a look in the linen draper's and see what they've got. And the haberdasher's, too, for some trims.'

'Yes, Aunt.'

Her aunt provided her with some guineas and told Clare to buy some black ribbon and some new trims for their bonnets.

Clare was only too pleased to go. She studied the gown of any well-dressed lady she passed and briefly looked in at a milliner's shop window, before spending some time looking at the swaths of cloths in a large linen draper's establishment.

There were so many dress fabrics to choose from and she tried to remember them to inform her aunt and was allowed a few fabric samples. At the haberdasher's she found many ribbons and trimmings to be able to select what she liked.

* * *

On the way home she passed Sylvester's Dancing Academy and decided it might well be a good establishment in which to learn to dance. But she decided to ask her aunt first before booking lessons, because by this time she was tired, and having bought some pretty edgings and black ribbons she didn't want to go into the dance studio laden with packages.

These activities pleased Clare very much. Especially anticipating meeting Captain Chatham again. She felt more alive, excited . . . and hopeful. But what she was hopeful for, she was not certain.

She presumed it was that she was hoping her aunt would find a suitable man to marry. But deep in her heart she suddenly realised it was not only her aunt she hoped would marry — but herself, also!

It was a shame Captain Chatham was against marriage. But she considered if he had intended to marry, then her aunt would have secured him. Or one of the fashionable ladies, who swarmed around the Spa looking for spouses for themselves or their unwed daughters, would snap him up.

'You have done well,' Aunt Maud cried, as she saw the fashion plates and trimmings Clare brought home. 'Now we must waste no time in deciding what we want as I must get some new gowns before I meet Colonel Rupert Rufus.'

Horror attacked Clare making her stutter. 'Colonel R . . . Rufus, Ma'am?' she gulped, 'I believe . . . I mean, army officers are not always trustworthy.'

'Oh, so you have heard of that silly rumour Captain Chatham told me about him? A scandal the Captain said I should ignore. Colonel Rufus is 'a fine fellow', he said. Although he's as poor as a church mouse. But being poor isn't a fault and that shouldn't colour my opinion of him.'

'Oh!' Clare said faintly.

4

In the morning, Clare awoke with her mind whirling as she thought of the happenings of the day before. Suddenly she felt no longer imprisoned forever as a companion to a rather dull lady. Her life seemed to have opened up with plenty of interest ahead of her.

Particularly, her thoughts were lit up by the image of Captain Chatham. She'd changed her opinion about him. She'd discovered his austere image hid a lively personality. And it was exciting to think she was going to see him again later that morning.

She also had enjoyable shopping trips and new clothes to look forward to, as well. The scoundrel officer who attacked Annie Willis had to be avoided, but that didn't deter her enthusiasm to go out. Finally, there was the prospect of learning to dance, which she was sure she would like.

But first she had to rise early as she remembered she had promised to meet Annie, the nursemaid. So she pushed back the bedcovers and rushed to her washstand.

★   ★   ★

A little later, in the sunshine, she hurried down the driveway of Knowle Park.

'I'm ever so pleased you've come,' said Annie, who was waiting for her with the pram by the Brocklehurst's stone gate-posts.

After cooing over baby Billy, and giving him some bread for the ducks — which he tried to eat himself — the girls trundled the pram towards the river bank.

'I'm scared of Hot Wells Lane now,' Annie confessed as they started to walk down it.

'You'll be safe with me,' Clare assured the little maid. 'Now I want to tell you that Captain Chatham is looking for the officer who attacked you. The Captain has already investigated one army officer who has a distinctive moustache and he tells me it can't be him. So he is looking for another officer with a long growth of hair on his upper lip. Can you remember anything else about him?'

'He was quick as lightning and very nimble on his feet. And although he was skinny he was quite strong too. He grabbed me from behind he did. I didn't really see his face because I was struggling to get away from him.'

'I'm meeting Captain Chatham later, Annie, and he would like to know, did you notice any colour apart from the scarlet of his coat? Were his lapels green or blue?'

'Are you funning? I was fighting for me life. I wasn't looking for bits of coloured cloth.'

Clare could understand her indignation and walked along thoughtfully. 'Was his uniform spruce?'

'What do you mean?'

'Did his uniform look clean? Were his boots polished?'

Annie screwed up her face as if thinking. 'I dunno. I can't remember. Oh yes, he weren't very clean. He smelled.'

'What of?' Clare asked quickly.

'Tobacco. Yes, it were tobacco, mainly.'

Clare made a mental note of that and then told Annie not to chatter about the attack to anyone.

'Acourse I won't blab. It were embarrassing. Besides I have my good name to protect. I'm to be married soon.'

Clare smiled at the nursemaid. 'I'm happy for you.'

Billy was delighted to see some ducks and Annie took him out of his pram so that he could stand and throw the bread into the water for them. They all laughed at the little boy's reaction to the ducks' antics. Soon it was time to return home.

'See you tomorrow,' Clare said waving goodbye and then almost ran back to Knowle Park for her breakfast.

To her surprise her aunt was up and waiting for her in the breakfast parlour.

Amazed to see the plump lady up at an early hour, Clare apologised for being late.

But Maud didn't seem to mind. 'Now, I have decided what gowns I would like and I want you to run down into Bristol and tell the modiste to pay me a visit today. Then I would like you to get me some more of the wide black ribbons you bought yesterday . . . '

Clare listened, trying to remember all the orders that were fired at her. It seemed an endless list, but Clare was happy to see her aunt motivated.

She wondered if she should mention that she was to meet Captain Chatham at eleven o'clock and decided that part of her life should be kept secret.

Armed with instructions, including a visit to the bank to draw out an enormous sum to pay for the purchases, Clare took the long way around the streets to avoid going down Hot Wells Lane alone.

Later, feeling tired from tramping around the town, she was pleased to spy the Captain's long figure sitting in the coffee room of the Hotwells Spa.

On seeing her he immediately rose, and bowed, impressing Clare that he could move so quickly, unaided by his stick. His stern expression melted as he said, 'Good morning, Miss Fountain. May I order you a cup of spa water? Or a cup of coffee? Or do you prefer a glass of lemonade? You look a little jaded.'

Not offended that he noted her flushed appearance after rushing about, Clare bobbed and smiled up at him. 'Yes, you are right I have been in practically all the shops in the town and would appreciate a glass of lemonade.' She sat down by him as he indicated.

'My aunt is keen to renovate her wardrobe — and mine.' She gave a little laugh, 'In double quick time.'

'Ah!' the Captain said. 'Men are lucky. They can get away with one or two good suits that serve them well for years. Far less fuss than bothering with fashion.'

Clare nodded thinking he had had to wear his naval uniform everyday in the Navy since he was a boy, and therefore saw no need for anything else. Although she was pleased to observe Captain Chatham had the appearance of a man who cared for personal grooming.

She could have let the subject rest, but she couldn't resist remarking, 'But sir, life would be very uninteresting for men if women didn't flaunt themselves a little. Clothes are one of ladies' pleasures. Now what do you think of me wearing a rose ball gown, or would a green suit my dark hair. I'm too old to wear pale coloured muslins.'

Amazed to find himself discussing female apparel, the Captain looked askance. Then his lips lifted as if he couldn't resist a smile. If there was one thing about Miss Fountain he liked, it was that he felt quite comfortable when he was with her.

He seemed quite at ease to discuss anything. 'Well now, I wouldn't call you too old for any colour,' he remarked, looking admiringly at her youthful figure and complexion.

In fact as Clare's bright eyes looked at his, Peter found himself reluctant to look away.

'I must order you a drink,' he said suddenly coming down to earth.

Sipping her lemonade a few moments later, Clare reported that Annie couldn't remember anything of her attacker's coloured lapels or cuffs. 'She was too scared,' Clare told the Captain.

'Quite so.'

Seeing he'd reverted to his normal reticence she was content to finish her drink and allow him to ponder.

'Well,' he said at last, 'so far I haven't been able to find the culprit, but I'm continuing to make enquiries. The fellow may have left the district. Frightened off by the whack on the head you gave him.'

She giggled. 'Yes, that is possible.'

'But in the meantime, take care not to walk alone anywhere he may be hiding and waiting for a young lady to come by.'

Clare assured him she would, then said, 'Now, I must go. I have one other thing to do before I return for lunch. Thank you for the drink.'

As she rose to leave, he rose too and surprising himself — as he could think of no reason to meet her — 'Come again tomorrow.'

Pleased, Clare said she would if she could.

'Oh, and ask your aunt when she wishes Colonel Rufus to call.'

'I will, sir,' she called over her shoulder as she quickly departed.

Peter sat down watching her neat figure disappear. For some time after she'd gone he wasn't aware of sitting in a pleasant trance.

Eventually he rose, and determined not to use his stick he tucked it over his arm. He whistled softly to himself as he strode out of the Spa buildings and gazed at the shipping on the shimmering Avon water as he walked gingerly but steadily along the sunny riverside path. He felt his life had, unexpectantly, taken a turn for the better — but he couldn't think why.

★　★　★

Clare's reason for rushing off wasn't that she minded being late for lunch. Or that she wanted to leave Captain Chatham. It was because she had to call at the Dance Academy and arrange to take some lessons.

She'd already noted the Captain wasn't one to waste time, and she didn't want to be taken to a ball and be unable to stand up and dance. Although she carried a few small packages from her shopping she felt she was not too cluttered today, having asked the shopkeepers to deliver the heavier items.

The Sylvester Dancing Academy looked like a Greek temple from the outside, and as Clare mounted the steps to the front entrance she could hear a fiddler playing a well-known dance tune.

Inside the hall, lit by tall side windows, some young girls and boys were being instructed in the steps of a Quadrille. At the far end of the dance studio was a platform where a wiry instructor was prancing about on his toes showing the class how they should move. He was obviously the dance master, Mr Sylvester.

The boys were clumsy and clopped on the floorboards while the girls became red-faced and giggled when making mistakes, but their instructor's tart verbal reminders and sharp taps with his long cane, managed to guide them through the dance until the violin player broke a string and the dancing stopped.

Clare had been fascinated by the spectacle as she stopped and watched, her feet itched to dance to the music. But during the pause while the violinist changed a string, the instructor, who noticed her standing at the door, called, 'Young lady, what is it you want?'

All eyes turned on Clare and she wished the floorboards would open up and she could disappear from their inquisitive gaze.

'I beg your pardon, interrupting your class, sir,' she said giving him a polite curtsey.

The dance master walked towards her with a fast springy step making her feel like an insect trapped in a spider's web.

'I would like to learn to dance,' Clare said, feeling uneasy although he gave her a wide smile and bowed in an exaggerated fashion.

As he assessed her, he took out a snuff box and using his finger and thumb removed a pinch and sniffed it into his nostril with his bony fingers raised like a fan. Quickly she stepped back as he sneezed and waved his lace-edged handkerchief in front of his nose. No doubt it was the refined way of taking snuff, but it did not impress Clare. Nor the way his eyes penetrated her figure, but she excused him thinking he was assessing if she would be able to dance.

'I have a beginners' class starting on Saturday. You may come to that.'

'What time is the class?'

He scratched under his wig. 'Five o'clock.'

Clare frowned. Five seemed rather late in the day. 'Have you an earlier time?' she asked.

His eyes narrowed. 'I teach school pupils during the day time. Young ladies like yourself should have learned to dance at school.'

'Yes, I know I should,' agreed Clare weakly. She didn't want to admit her parents couldn't afford dancing classes for her when she was young. 'I'll come at five,' she agreed, 'and will you send the bill to Lady Hadfield at Clifton please.'

'Are you her daughter?'

'No, sir, I'm her companion.'

He gave a twisted smile. 'Ah yes.' He looked down at her worn shoes and said, 'and get some dance slippers before you come.'

'Yes, sir.'

Clare was dismissed and felt almost glad to get out of the place. Mr Sylvester was intimidating. As he slithered away he reminded her of a snake. Then she shook herself. What did it matter if she disliked him? He was willing to teach her to dance, and from the little she'd seen of him dancing she judged him to be very good at it.

★ ★ ★

Maud was delighted with her shopping and said so when they sat down for lunch. 'Clare I almost feel like going down to the shops myself, they seemed to have such good stocks of things nowadays.'

'I think you should,' Clare agreed.

Maud mused out loud, 'I could park my carriage in Wine Street then I wouldn't have far to walk to the shops, would I?'

'Indeed, Ma'am,' Clare nodded pleased to think her aunt was willing to take even a few steps out.

After discussing the shops that would be easy to visit, Clare mentioned meeting Captain Chatham.

'The Captain would like to know when he should ask Colonel Rufus to call on you.'

'Oh well, it depends when the dressmakers can get me fitted out.'

Clare considered when it came to matrimony it was the person you married that mattered, not what they wore, but she didn't say so. She suggested, 'Shall I reply in a week or two?'

'Are you going to see the Captain again?'

'Yes Ma'am. I have to get a reply to him, don't I?'

Maud took a forkful of food and

chewed it slowly. Swallowing, she said, 'Yes I suppose you'll have to let him know so that the Colonel is informed he must wait.'

* * *

Having the excuse to see Captain Chatham made it easy for Clare to slip away next morning and to meet him at the coffee room.

It was nice to see his familiar figure. He seemed to be waiting for her at the same table they'd had the day before.

'Ah, Miss Fountain,' he said coming towards her and bowing. 'Do come and sit down.'

After ordering a coffee, he asked, 'What news have you today?'

Although there were other people partaking of refreshment it seemed to Clare that they could ignore them and she began telling him quietly, that her aunt wanted a week or two to prepare herself to meet Colonel Rufus. Then, seeing he was a good listener, she went on to tell him about the arrangement she'd made for taking dancing classes. 'I feel a little uneasy,' she admitted, 'going by myself at that hour of the day.'

The Captain smiled, 'Well I think I can help you there.'

Clare's questioning expression made him go on to explain that he, too, was thinking of learning to dance. 'We shall go together,' he said. 'And may I apologise in advance if I trip over as I am still a little unsteady on my pins?'

Clare assured him she would understand it would be difficult for him but she beamed saying, 'I think it's splendid we are taking dance classes together.'

5

When Saturday came, Clare began the day enjoying a walk with Annie and baby William. After breakfast she was sent on several errands by her aunt. Then shopping trips. Maud thought nothing of making Clare run down to the shops again and again if she wanted to change some merchandise or thought of something else she wanted.

'I could do with a pair of wheels on my feet,' Clare remarked breathlessly to Captain Chatham as they met for their daily coffee.

'Well, I for one am pleased your Aunt Maud is so demanding. These constant trips to town give me the opportunity to enjoy a coffee with you each morning.'

Peter hid a little gasp. He'd confessed he appreciated the company of a lady, which was entirely against his belief that he was uneasy in the company of women. So he added quickly, 'I have seen Mr Sylvester and arranged to take daily class with you starting this evening.'

Clare felt a little apprehensive about her first dance class. From what she'd seen of Mr Sylvester he appeared to be an exacting teacher. But now she was comforted to think Captain Chatham would be with her.

And instead of worrying she might fall over his large feet, it was more likely he would fall over hers.

'Did Mr Sylvester tell you to get some dance shoes?'

'He did. And I informed him I was none too steady on my feet, so he said he would dance any intricate steps with you.'

'Oh dear me. I fear I will show I have wooden feet. Mr Sylvester prances about like a marionette.'

They both laughed making other coffee drinkers turn to see what had amused them. Previously Clare had ignored other people in the Spa coffee room when she was with the Captain, but suddenly she recollected Society wouldn't ignore them, especially her behaviour. Ladies often had little better to do with their time than to criticise and vie with one another. They would have noticed her meetings with Captain Chatham so she'd better not forget that she was on show.

Any one of them could mention their meetings to Aunt Maud and how would her Ladyship react? Would Maud be angry, or even jealous of her frequently seeing the Captain?

Consequently, aware of creating a minor disturbance in the polite company of the coffee room, Clare made the effort to steady her hand and pick up her cup attempting to drink soberly, while Peter quickly composed himself too, and said, 'I have a message for you to deliver.'

Clare put down her coffee cup. It was delicious coffee because the Captain always made sure she had it served just as she liked it, not too strong and not too weak. 'Yes, sir?'

'Colonel Rufus is a little impatient of waiting for her Ladyship's invitation for him to call and is intending to present himself at Knowle Park tomorrow afternoon at three o'clock.'

'Oh! I don't know if she'll like that. Being told, I mean.'

Peter grinned. 'She may not. But sooner or later she will discover that Colonel Rupert Rufus is a man of resolve as well as bravery. He won't be pushed around by any lady. Indeed, he will soon make it clear to your aunt that if she is not prepared to rise from that couch of hers, then he will be off.'

Clare chuckled. 'My aunt is used to giving orders not receiving them. He sounds as if he might be just the right man for her.'

'We shall see. But I hope so, otherwise she'll be after me again.'

They smiled at each other. Yet Clare was appalled to think the Captain might yet be captured in marriage by

Maud. Her aunt wouldn't suit him and living in the same house with him married to Maud would be intolerable for her. Oddly, she was beginning to think of the Captain as her friend now.

As they rose to part, she asked if he had had any luck with discovering the identity of Annie's attacker.

'No, I haven't,' he said gravely, 'but I've heard another young woman was attacked in Bristol last night.'

'Oh dear me! When? Where?'

'In St Augustine's churchyard near College Green. A young schoolteacher was making her way home and was followed.'

He didn't go on to explain what had happened, but Clare feared the worst. 'Oh! St Augustine's is not far from here,' she said with a shudder.

'Yes indeed. I fear that man, whoever he is, is still being a menace. The only difference I understand was that it was not a soldier who attacked her. He was, the poor woman reported, dressed in a farmer's smock.'

Clare was puzzled. That seemed to rule out the possibility of the attacker being the officer who attacked Annie. 'Perhaps it was not the same man?' she suggested.

'That is possible. Regiments move camp. Although I don't understand why a farm worker would come into town to attack a woman.'

This frank conversation with a man might have made Clare blush a few weeks ago, but she was so used to talking freely with the Captain she didn't seem to mind what they discussed.

'I see what you mean,' she said slowly. 'There's some mystery about it.'

'So, to protect you, I will come and collect you from Knowle Park this evening and I'll take you home.'

'But, Captain, you can't walk all that way and have a dance session as well!' exclaimed Clare.

'I don't intend to. I shall drive my carriage.'

'Oh,' Clare said wondering if she was

in danger of being told off by her aunt at being taken to the dance class in the Captain's carriage. 'I'll walk down the driveway and wait for you at the gate-keeper's cottage,' she said.

Whether he knew why she didn't want him to pick her up at the front door of Knowle Park, she wasn't sure, but he nodded as if he was happy to oblige.

Maud was furious to learn the Colonel was intending to come and see her the next day.

'What a cheek!' she cried, getting up from her chaise-longue and swishing about the drawing-room in her negligee. 'What am I supposed to wear? My new wardrobe isn't finished yet. You'll have to spend the afternoon sewing the lace on that mauve gown of mine, Clare.'

'Yes, Aunt, I will,' Clare said pleasantly, but she became anxious worrying about keeping Captain Chatham waiting at the end of the driveway at a quarter to five. 'May I be excused dinner this evening as I have a dance class arranged?'

'Miss dinner?' Maud looked horrified.

'I don't mind,' Clare assured her.

'Very well. I will get cook to leave you a cold supper for when you get in.'

'Thank you, aunt. Now, if you will excuse me I must get on with sewing on your lace trim.'

★ ★ ★

Clare was hard pushed to get the sewing finished by the time she had to change for her dance class, but she managed it. She hadn't had the time to make more than one new walking-out gown for herself, as she'd been so busy with her aunt's things.

She had no evening gown, so she chose a loose-fitting summer dress that she'd worn a great deal in her younger, plumper days, and put her old wool cloak over her dress thinking she didn't look well-dressed.

In fact, she was ashamed to be so

poorly attired especially as the Captain she knew would be well turned out. She carried her new dance slippers as she didn't want to ruin them wearing them walking outside.

She almost ran down the long drive.

Exactly at the time he said he would arrive, Captain Chatham's carriage appeared. Clare smiled. The Captain was so reliable. It was nice to think she could trust him.

There were a few other people assembled at the dance studio: a merry young couple, a newly-rich tradesman and his portly wife, anxious to learn the social graces, and a rather stiff young lady who looked as though she was there under protest.

Mr Sylvester took control of his motley group easily, and began by getting them to stand tall saying, 'Correct deportment is essential.' He went around the room poking them into shape. Then he got them to walk in a circle while he stood in the middle watching and making almost bullying comments to improve their movements. Next he got everyone to bend their knees, and the men to bow and the ladies to curtsey gracefully.

'Now we will learn the five dance positions,' he said springing up on to the raised platform so they could all see his feet.

'Position one. Toes out, like so,' called Mr Sylvester in his shrill voice, demonstrating how they should hold their arms, and hands, too.

The clumsy members of the class did their best. Although Clare found it easier than most. A quick glance at the Captain told her he was finding it an ordeal but he was managing beautifully. He noticed her looking at him and grimaced. She hoped her smile back gave him encouragement.

'Now, the second position, toes to the side,' the instructor's voice rang out. 'Then, the third, to the front.' There was something about his voice that Clare recollected but she couldn't think where she'd heard it before.

When one foot had to cross in front of the other, some of the class found it difficult. Fortunately, Clare found it came naturally to her.

Then came the complicated bit, learning the steps and movements of a country dance.

Concentrating on the instruction, Clare was only able to glance once or twice at the Captain who was having more difficulty than she in balancing, but was doing it as best he could and he grinned at her when he caught her looking at him.

They went through the patterns and steps of two well-known country dances before the fiddler was brought into play the tunes while the learner dancers attempted to remember all the instructions.

Mr Sylvester stalked around tapping their feet into the correct position with his long cane. Clare felt quite scared of him, but he told her, 'You are my star pupil.'

'I for one, am not sorry the class has

ended,' remarked the Captain, clearly suffering from the exertion. 'I can only hope in time dancing will be less of a punishment and provide pleasure as it does for many people.'

Clare looked at him sympathetically. 'I have to admit I enjoyed the session, although being very much younger than you, and not afflicted with injuries, it has been less of an ordeal for me.'

'Quite so,' Peter remarked wryly. He was suffering from physical pain after the unaccustomed exercise, which he was trying to hide, but the added blow of being told he was ancient — when he was aged thirty, only six or seven years older than Miss Fountain — was hard to bear.

Did he really present himself as a greybeard to her? It was quite worrying.

Determined to find out where he stood in her eyes, Peter asked her in the carriage going back to Knowle Park. 'Do I seem old to you, Miss Fountain?'

As it was becoming dark, her eyes glittered in the dim light of the carriage.

'Old?' she repeated. 'Old for what?'

The word, marriage, came into his head. He dismissed it instantly. 'I mean, do you consider I'm . . . a man passed his prime?'

'Good heavens, no, sir.' She sat and scrutinised him, thinking she was being drawn into the web of his goodness, charm and good manners. She couldn't tell him that though. 'I think,' she said, 'you have a lot to offer.'

'Who?'

'Well,' she shrugged. 'If my aunt takes to Colonel Rufus then you have the choice of many widows and young ladies looking out for an eligible gentleman like yourself.'

'Ah!' Peter sank back on to the squabs, content that she thought him still worthy of being considered a good catch.

'Of course,' added Clare a little mischievously, 'If you persist in believing you are better off in the bachelor state . . . '

'I do,' he said firmly.

Clare gave an involuntary sigh. 'Thank you for the lift,' she said when they arrived at the gatekeeper's cottage.

'I shall take you up the driveway,' Peter said, thinking he wanted to prolong having her with him as long as possible. As well as noting it was getting dark and he didn't want her walking up the long drive alone.

'Thank you, sir.' And as the carriage bowled up the tree-lined drive she explained, 'I must apologise for my dress. I have some new materials to make some new clothes but never seem to have the time to sew them up. What with my aunt sending me errands all day long, and she has piles of sewing for me to do for her in the evenings, too.'

Peter assured her he understood. 'Young lady, you don't have to explain your difficulties. I understand your position, but I also think you bear it well. Very well indeed . . . ' He bent his head towards hers. 'Now we have arrived. Good night, God bless.'

He amazed himself to find his lips

coming closer to hers — and she did not seem to mind the intimacy. It seemed right for them to kiss.

Their kiss had been warm and brief. But as he struggled with his legs — which were sore after dancing — to get out of the carriage and escort her to the door, his inclination was to take her in his arms and kiss her again. But she was too quick for him and darted up the front door steps only to turn and wave before letting herself in the door.

But her heart was pounding as she shut the door and leant back against it.

With her hand on her bosom, she waited for her breath to become quieter before she removed her cloak and entered the drawing-room lit with many candles.

'I can't see him again, not after that kiss,' Clare's mutter showed she was feeling unsettled. 'I am a paid companion. I can't be putting myself forward. Anyway he told me he does not want to marry — and I'm certainly not going to be his mistress.'

She took a few deep breaths to try and calm herself. She enjoyed his kiss very much, but that was not the issue. Captain Chatham was probably like most sailors, on the look out for any woman.

Normally though, he hadn't struck her as a womaniser. And you could usually tell the type of men that were.

'Well,' she told herself quietly, 'I shall not see him again. I have no need to. I have no more messages to take or deliver.'

Then she put her hand over her mouth with a gasp. 'Oh dear, I will have to. In my dither as he kissed me I left my dance slippers in his carriage.'

'Clare, is that you?' her aunt's voice called from the drawing-room, and Clare knew she could not escape to her bedchamber. She would have to go and talk to her.

'How did you get on?' Maud enquired from her reclined position on her chaise-longue.

'Oh, very well I think, for a first lesson.'

'Mmm. I expect you're young enough to jig and bob about quite easily. I couldn't do it.'

Clare said diplomatically. 'Well, I think you could, Aunt. We didn't do much dancing. We were just shown how to stand and walk. And then, how to bow,' she gave a demonstration curtsey, 'and the five dance positions for our feet. Afterwards we went through a country dance set.'

'We? Who was there?'

Clare felt her face warm. She gulped. 'Oh, there were half a dozen of us,' she said airily, anxious not to mention Captain Chatham. She went on, 'Mr Sylvester said we did quite well.'

Maud sniffed. 'Well, I'm glad to hear it. Now, run along and find the cold platter that Cook has left for you in the kitchen.'

Clare felt guilty as she went for her supper. She didn't know if she was being deceitful avoiding telling her aunt about herself and the Captain.

It was kind of her aunt to remember she hadn't eaten, but she couldn't eat much of the meal. She felt far too jumpy inside. The Captain had kissed her and sent her feelings in disarray. Yet it probably didn't mean much to him. Men, she'd been told, were unlikely to place any importance on a quick goodbye kiss. Yet for her, it was a magical moment she would never forget.

6

Daylight invaded Clare's bedroom too soon the next morning, as her aching feet told her it was too early to get up. But she had to rise and was soon ready for her early morning walk with Annie.

Baby William had become fond of her and lisped, 'Care,' because he couldn't say Clare.

He sat in his pram and waved his arms at her frantically until she gave him a kiss, and some bread to feed the ducks.

'Annie, you must be looking forward to having some children of your own after looking after someone else's,' Clare remarked.

'Yes, I am,' Annie agreed. 'And I hope they are as good as Billy. He's an angel.'

'I'm sure you'll love them anyway, even if they are little terrors,' replied

Clare, thinking she, too, would like to have a child to love. But marriage was necessary and Annie had her man already waiting for her.

'Annie,' Clare asked the little nurse-maid tentatively, 'you have fallen in love which is lovely, but have you ever met a man who was not keen to marry?'

Annie gave a little hoot of laughter. 'None of 'em want to marry. You have to persuade them. You know, flirt a little.'

'Oh!' Clare gasped, never having thought of that.

Annie looked at Clare critically. 'You shouldn't find it difficult to get a man if that's what you're thinking. A pretty girl like you should find it easy.'

'Yes, but what if they are dead set against getting married?'

'Chose another man, then.'

Clare walked on in silence looking at the silver ribbon of river water. How magnificent the Avon was. But so was Captain Chatham!

Annie suddenly piped up. 'Oh, I see

you have fallen for someone!'

Clare protested. 'No I haven't.'

Annie giggled. 'Yes you have, or you wouldn't be asking me questions about it. Now why won't he marry? Is he taken by someone else?'

Clare shook her head. 'I don't know why he's so against marriage. In any case, he's a gentleman of means. I'm just a paid companion.'

'So what? If you can make him happy, and he can make you happy that's all that matters. You aren't asking him to become a butler, or a coachman, are you?'

Clare's face lit up with a smile. 'No, you're right, Annie. But he can't ask me to marry him if he intends to remain a bachelor.'

'Why can't he? People change their minds.'

'Well, because . . . I'm not sure why he is so dead set against marriage.'

Annie frowned. 'From what you tell me it seems you and him get on well together. You should ask him. Give it a try, gel. You'll never know if you don't ask, will you?'

Clare could have said that you couldn't talk to an austere man like the Captain about such matters, but she knew in her heart she'd found out he was most tender underneath, and she could talk to him about anything. Perhaps she would get around to discussing his attitude to marriage one day.

Walking back to Knowle Park a little later, Clare reasoned she shouldn't feel guilty she was seeing so much of Captain Chatham. And even thinking she might be a little in love with him, because her aunt seemed to be becoming attached to Colonel Rufus. So she needn't worry.

However, she would make it clear to the Captain she didn't attach any importance to his kiss. But she would endeavour to make herself some nice new clothes, even if it meant she had to stay up all night to sew them.

And she wouldn't meet him again

until she'd something nice to wear. He could bring her dance slippers to the next class.

What she didn't expect was to see Captain Chatham's carriage parked outside the gate keeper's cottage as she approached.

On seeing her coming, he stepped out of the carriage gingerly. 'Ouch! The pain!' He complained so bitterly Clare rushed up to assist him.

'That dancing class yesterday has almost killed me!' he moaned, rubbing his legs.

'Get back in the carriage, then,' said Clare, concerned at the pain etched on his face.

'Can't give in to it, Clare. Have to beat it.'

'Well, I must admit my feet were sore this morning, too, but having been for a walk with Annie and the baby, they feel all right now.'

He tried his best to smile at her. 'I'm off to the Spa and hope the water will ease my aching joints. I just came round with your dancing slippers you left in the carriage. I didn't want you to worry you'd lost them.'

She looked at his eyes, she hadn't meant to as it made her almost melt inside. 'Thank you, sir.'

'Peter,' he corrected her, not taking his eyes off her.

'Very well, I'll call you Peter, when we are together. But I'd like you to remember it is necessary for me — and you — to be formal in company. Especially my aunt, who employs me as her companion.'

'Quite so.'

Handing Clare the dance slippers his warm fingers accidentally touched her and she temporarily lost control of her mind. She stood in a pleasant trance. But Peter bowed then climbed back into his carriage.

He called to her, 'Shall I see you tomorrow?'

'I don't think I shall have a message for you . . . ' she was going to say, sir, but let the word die on her tongue.

Peter thought frantically for a reason to make her come. 'I, er, have a message for you ... ah yes, ask your aunt if she would like me to get tickets for the next assembly rooms ball.'

'But you are not in a fit state to dance.'

He sat down in his carriage and picked up the reins ready to drive off. 'Oh, the tickets are for herself and Colonel Rufus.'

Clare looked puzzled.

'But how can she tell? She doesn't meet the Colonel until this afternoon.'

Seeing his error the Captain leaned forward and said to Clare quietly, 'Then we shall go to the ball, eh?' He drove off before Clare could reply.

Tripping down the driveway, Clare smiled to herself. There was no doubt about it, he did seem to like her as much as she liked him.

He was clearly making an excuse for her to meet him at the coffee room. If only he was not so against marriage!

★ ★ ★

Colonel Rufus walked up from the town because he hadn't a carriage and couldn't afford to hire one.

Clare felt nervous on seeing him in his scarlet coat and white breeches as it reminded her of the man who attacked Annie. And when he stroked his long moustache she felt alarmed to think the Captain could be wrong and the Colonel could be the attacker.

But his manner was not that of a man who wanted to bully or harm women. He possessed courteous manners and charm as well as being down-to-earth.

He bowed to Aunt Maud and to Clare because her aunt had insisted she stay in the drawing-room as the Colonel was shown in.

'Will you take a dish of tea?' Aunt Maud suggested.

'Certainly,' replied the colonel. 'And I'll take a seat, too, if I may, it's been a long walk up from the town.'

Maud seemed a little taken aback by his forward manner but she could not take her eyes off him.

97

'You have a fine house here, Ma'am,' the Colonel remarked, looking around the huge room. 'Some fine pictures, I see.'

'Indeed,' Maud agreed, 'my late husband was fond of art.'

'And what do you like?'

Maud blinked. 'Nothing in particular, I'm afraid. I've never really thought about it.'

'So, I will have to get you out and we shall see the world and find out what you do like, eh, Ma'am?'

Clare hid a smile at her aunt's expression. She could tell her aunt was both repelled by the idea of leaving the comfort of her chaise-longue and yet fascinated to have the opportunity to do something interesting.

Maud asked, 'Where do you suggest we go?'

The Colonel gave an alarming roar of laughter, which made the ladies look at him intently. 'Well now, 'Ma'am. I will draw up some places of interest and you can choose which we will visit. I presume we may use your carriage? I regret to say I haven't one.'

'Of course,' Maud said timidly.

Clare might have been alarmed at the Colonel being so much in charge of the situation except he gave her a courteous smile as she gave him his cup of tea.

Consequently, Clare formed the opinion that she didn't disapprove of the Colonel. And her aunt was interested in going out and about with him. Which was a good thing, and certainly better than Maud lounging around all day long.

So in the next few weeks Lady Hadfield and Colonel Rufus, with Clare in attendance, were to be seen driving here and there on excursions in and around Bristol. Clare got used to hearing her aunt telling her that Rupert and she were off to Bath, or to view a great house or a cathedral or even to picnic at some picturesque country spot.

Clare found the outings as interesting as her aunt, but she was becoming very tired. She endeavoured to rush down to the Spa coffee room every day to see the Captain and to report on how her aunt and Colonel Rufus were getting on together. Then as well as accompanying them on their outings, she had her daily dancing lessons and was up half the night sewing.

So she was not surprised when Maud remarked, 'My dear Clare, you looked tired out. Has all the travelling about been too much for you?'

'Oh no. It is just that I seem to have so much sewing to do.'

'Poor child. Why didn't you say? We shall hire a sewing maid.'

'Thank you, Ma'am, I should appreciate some help.'

'Then you will find a good seamstress. And today you must rest. I can go out with Colonel Rufus by myself. I am quite used to him now and do not require you to come.'

Clare was pleased.

She told Captain Chatham when she next met him at the Spa coffee room. 'I think my aunt has found a good match in Colonel Rufus. She is becoming more alive and is enjoying the outings he plans. They are to go out together today without me.'

Peter smiled as he ordered them another cup of coffee as Clare was in no hurry to rush away as she used to. 'That is splendid. Has she mentioned to you that the Colonel is short of funds?'

'Not exactly, although I noted he had no money when we went out together, so my aunt always pays for everything. She didn't seem to mind.'

'I did warn her he was broke.'

Clare looked at his familiar face and smiled. 'It is just as well to be honest. It saves a lot of unpleasantness if people are able to understand each other.'

Peter called the waitress and asked for more coffee to be poured, and when she left their table he said, 'Ah yes. You are right. For your aunt and the Colonel there must be nothing hidden if they are to be happily married.'

Clare felt prompted to ask, 'So why

are you so against marriage?'

He spluttered as he drank and had to put his coffee cup down hurriedly, 'I? Well I suppose it is because I don't think I am cut out for it. I lived for years with only male company on board ship — '

'That's no excuse. Sailors marry.'

'I suppose they do.'

'Peter, of course they do. You are as fixed in your ways as my aunt was.'

He didn't like that comparison. 'I'm not just lazing around on a chaise-longue. I'm working hard at recovering from my injuries.'

Clare said a little unkindly, 'You're using that as an excuse. Why you walk around for miles and are learning to dance very well. That's no reason to give for being obstinate about marriage.'

Peter looked crestfallen and Clare felt ashamed of herself for scolding him, so she added, 'I think you have overcome your injuries very bravely. And my concern about you is no more than I should like to see you getting out and about as my aunt and Colonel Rufus do now.' She leant forward and asked quietly, 'Are you short of funds too?'

He laughed. 'No. I'm worth at least as much as your aunt is.'

Amazed, Clare's mouth opened. 'But, but I don't understand. You have no grand clothes, or servants, and even your carriage is ordinary.'

'I prefer to live simply. I'm used to it. I have all I need.'

'Not quite.'

He looked at her until she blushed. 'Young lady. Do I understand you think I need a wife?'

She almost shouted at him, yes, you do. But Clare refused to answer. She rose from the table saying, 'It's getting late. I must run.'

Clare had the uncomfortable feeling Peter knew she was just getting away from him fast because she didn't want to say she thought he needed a wife, or to reveal her deep feelings for him.

With her heart pounding at a furious

beat she walked off hearing him say, 'Even if it makes you late, don't walk down Hot Wells Lane. It is dangerous.'

What she didn't realise was that Peter too, was feeling a heightened sense of emotion though he barely hid it. Her recently acquired new clothes had turned her into a beauty in his eyes. She was a treasure. A woman he had grown to know and like very much.

She'd raised some hidden feelings he had buried in his unconsciousness. His insistence on remaining a bachelor had given him a shield. Now he knew he must face up to those natural desires.

Every evening for the past few weeks he'd driven her home after the dance classes, and every evening he'd kissed her goodnight, and recently those kisses had become something he'd looked forward to. Was he being like his hero, Lord Nelson, who claimed he couldn't see because he'd put his telescope to his blind eye?

As he strode back to his house he felt it was empty. Something was missing.

Perhaps Clare was right — he needed a lady around his house.

* * *

It was sheer mulishness that made Clare walk down Hot Wells Lane alone. She felt so cross with Peter and his silly excuses for saying he would never marry, that she wanted to disobey him.

She felt the urge to prove him wrong about the danger of walking down Hot Wells Lane alone too. She didn't have to obey his orders!

So she determinedly set off to go down the lane. It was much quicker than going the long way around the streets.

Seeing the red coat of Colonel Rufus ahead, with his long moustache, she ran along the path to catch him up to him, calling, 'Colonel, how pleased I am to see you!' She added breathlessly, 'Are you walking up to Knowle Park to see my aunt?'

It was not until she reached him and

he turned around so that she could see him properly, that she realised that the officer was not Colonel Rufus!

'Ah, Miss Fountain. How fortunate to meet you,' exclaimed her dance master, Mr Sylvester, with his glittering eyes fixed on her.

7

Mr Sylvester!' gasped Clare, surprised and disappointed it wasn't Colonel Rufus.

She stepped back as he came up with a fast step but he didn't bow as she was sure Colonel Rufus would have done. 'Well, well. Miss Fountain. Out enjoying a stroll? Don't you ever do any work for your employer?'

He was not to know Lady Hadfield treated her more like a daughter than a servant. Besides, it was none of his business where she went, or what she did.

'I didn't expect you to be dressed in an officer's uniform,' she said trying not to sound annoyed. 'I thought you were someone else I know. He has a similar moustache.'

Blocking her way, his eyes slid from right to left. 'I don't expect you know I take part in theatricals,' Mr Sylvester said in his high sing-song voice. 'I like dressing up.'

'Oh!' exclaimed Clare, not knowing what to say. Of course he was only in a play costume.

Anyway, she knew Colonel Rufus would never venture out with his uniform looking crumpled or dirty, poor though he was. And he had a button missing. Colonel Rufus would have sewn a missing button on.

Trying to sound less annoyed than she was to be held back, Clare asked, 'Which production are you in, sir?'

'We are rehearsing at the moment,' he told her.

It seemed reasonable that he was an actor as well as a dance instructor, and that his part in the play meant that he had to wear a soldier's uniform, so he had fixed a huge moustache on his face. There was probably a hall nearby — although Clare couldn't think of one — where Mr Sylvester was going to a play rehearsal because he was walking away from the direction of the Bristol Theatre.

He put out his hand to touch her but she drew away. 'Mr Sylvester, I must pick a few bluebells to take home,' she said, saying the first thing she could think of to get away from him.

'Dear me,' she exclaimed, glancing at the woods and seeing the brown dried heads of the flowers, 'I promised to bring my aunt some but I see they are over. Well, I must rush, my aunt is expecting me for dinner.'

Even that excuse to get away from him was not a good one, as it was midday, so she added lamely, 'I mean, Lady Hadfield is expecting me for lunch,' knowing her aunt had gone out for a day's excursion with Colonel Rufus.

She wished Mr Sylvester hadn't come up so close to her, as she could smell his unpleasant stale snuff. 'Come into the woods and we will see if we can find another flower we can pick for your aunt,' he said, trying this time to take hold of her elbow but she twisted away from him.

In a quandary what to do or say, Clare was only aware that she wanted to flee. Mr Sylvester was a good dance master and had taught her well, but there was something about him she didn't like.

'No, thank you. I must go,' she muttered again, avoiding his sharp eyes.

She had the horrific feeling that even if she took to her toes and ran, he would be swifter and would soon catch her up.

To her relief he stepped aside saying, 'Very well. I shall see you later at your dance class.'

Clare had to agree that she would be there. 'Yes, Mr Sylvester, Captain Chatham kindly comes to collect me in his carriage.'

'Does he now.'

She couldn't get out of the lane fast enough and practically ran all the way up the hill to Clifton, arriving exhausted.

'Why, Miss Fountain,' exclaimed

Cook, looking at the panting young lady. 'What's the mad rush for? Her Ladyship won't be back until about seven o'clock she said, and I was to set out a cold platter of meats in the dining-room for your lunch.'

'Thank you,' endeavouring to smile as her breathing became easier, 'I wasn't sure of the time.'

★ ★ ★

Lunch calmed her down, and afterwards when the new seamstress arrived she was occupied telling the girl what to sew. She found the time went quickly and it was soon time for Clare to change into her dance gown and meet Captain Chatham at the gatekeeper's cottage.

Nervous of meeting Peter as she had practically lost her temper with him over his refusal to tell her why he was so against marriage, Clare prepared to meet him again in trepidation. But it was not only that disagreement between

111

them she had to repair, there was something else, more important, which made her anxious to see him: her suspicions about Mr Sylvester. Therefore, she made sure she wasn't late, and when she saw the carriage coming along the road earlier than usual she was glad she wouldn't be keeping him waiting.

But it was not his carriage that came along to take her to the dance class. It was a hackney carriage.

As the carriage drew up beside her she saw Captain Chatham was not in the carriage. Had he taken umbrage to her impertinent questions about his private life?

Was he so annoyed with her that he was refusing to come and collect her in his carriage for the dance class?

'Miss Fountain?'

Clare nodded. She felt the fellow rude not to attempt to get down and open the carriage door for her. 'Hop in,' said the driver said brusquely, 'I've been told to collect you.'

He hardly gave her time to be seated before he whipped the horse to trot down the road.

*   *   *

As she sat alone in the musty coach, Clare became nervous. How she regretted her questioning about Peter's private affairs. Had this made a permanent rift between them?

Surely not! She couldn't imagine Captain Chatham would be so petty. And she seemed to remember it was she who had become annoyed, not him. Maybe he was unwell this evening, or for some reason he was unable to attend the class and was unable to collect her.

It was most aggravating, as she particularly wanted to tell him of her growing unease about Mr Sylvester. Especially as she'd remembered the gilt button she'd picked up when Annie had been attacked, and Mr Sylvester had a button missing from his play costume.

Her nervousness grew as she noticed the carriage was not taking her directly to The Sylvester Dance Academy. They were going down Park Street towards the docks.

'Driver!' she called out after opening the carriage window, 'You are going the wrong way to the Dance Academy.' But either the driver didn't hear her or he didn't want to.

The carriage bowled on at a fast pace and Clare struggled to understand what was going on. She put her head as far out of the window as she dared and called again, 'Driver, where are you taking me?'

He seemed determined to ignore her.

She then strained to see someone she could call out to, saying she was being taken where she didn't want to go. But as it was time for most people's evening meal there seemed to be few people about, and none near enough for her to attract their attention as the carriage moved fast along the street.

Panic rose in Clare's breast. There

was something definitely wrong about the driver's behaviour. He was deliberately ignoring her calls to stop. She was being taken to the dockland area, which was a notorious place for vagabonds and thieves. No young lady in her right senses would go there unaccompanied.

A sudden urge made Clare decide she must get out of the coach, and when the driver slowed a little to round a bend before entering a yard, she opened the door and jumped.

How the fall hurt. But so anxious was she to hide, she ignored the battering her body received and crawled for safety behind some barrels.

It was just as well as the carriage came to halt and she heard men's voices.

'I got her mate, in the carriage.'

'But she ain't there!'

'What do yer mean, she ain't there?'

Curses followed as the two men found the carriage empty.

'Sylvester won't like it.'

There, thought Clare shivering from

her hiding place. She had suspected Mr Sylvester might be a rogue. And now she had proof he had tried to kidnap her!

She froze in fear as she heard the men curse. 'She can't be far away. I heard her yell and scream at me to stop not five minutes ago. Search for her. She can't have got far. I need that money Sylvester promised me for getting her.'

Where could Clare go? Nowhere. The barrels offered her protection, but there seemed no other hiding place nearby.

She could feel her mouth dry but her hands had become sweaty. She was bound to be found as the men moved around looking for her. And then what would happen to her?'

With a pounding heart she prayed for help.

When she heard a sudden piercing squeal she looked up and saw the two men were apprehending another girl, who must have been passing by. 'Let me go, you brutes!' the accosted girl screamed.

The poor girl's cries made Clare feel helpless and cruel. She daren't go to assist the victim, knowing she would be caught too. As the men knocked the girl out and dragged her body off to a warehouse, Clare saw the opportunity to run.

How she blessed her fitness and ability to fly down the dock's road. Terrified at any moment the men might realise they had kidnapped the wrong girl she ran on hoping she would soon come to an area she recognised.

Coming to the bridge that she remembered the carriage taking, she flew over it and soon she was heaving for breath as her chest ached but saw houses ahead.

A hand bell was being rung and Clare spotted a street vendor selling his wares.

'Steady on, Missy,' the pieman said as she rushed up to him, 'Me pies ain't all gone yet. There's one for you.'

Clare was so breathless she could only shake her head, trying to get the breath to reply. 'Where . . . where am I?'

'Right here. Now how many pies do you want? As it's the end of the day I'll give you two for a shilling. Now don't keep shaking your head, lass. That's as good a bargain as you'll find anywhere.'

'I'm sorry,' spluttered Clare, 'I don't want . . . a pie,' she took a huge breath, 'I must find Brandon Hill. Quickly.'

'Brandon Hill? Well it's been there for years so I doubt if it has moved.'

'Which direction will I find it?' Clare asked desperately.

The pieman, knowing he was not going to sell the last of his pies to the harassed young lady, pointed with his finger and moved on, clanging his bell.

Clare having had a short rest, flew in the direction the pieman had indicated and was relieved to find herself in a part of town she recognised.

'Whew!' she stopped by a railing and held on to it for support while gaining her breath and mopping her brow.

An elegant lady and gentleman strolling by looked at her haughtily.

Clare could have asked for their assistance, but they didn't look as if they were the kind of people who would be quick to understand her predicament. Or to be willing to help her as they would judge her by her appearance and Clare knew she now must look dishevelled as well as exhausted.

Her best bet was to go to the Dance Academy — although she was now terrified of seeing Mr Sylvester and must avoid him at all cost — and find Captain Chatham. Peter might still be cross with her but she was sure he would act promptly to have the girl at the docks released before any harm came to her. And as Peter was seeking the man who'd attacked Annie Willis, and now it seemed Mr Sylvester was that man, she had to tell him.

★ ★ ★

At last she reached the dancing school but she hesitated at the entrance. Dare she go in?

She had to.

'Put your arms, so. Take four skips forward . . . ' Sylvester's strident voice from the dance hall sent a shudder of fear through Clare when she heard it.

She must look in the hall, although Sylvester might see her and then what would she do? It was a nightmare but she had to pluck up the courage to look.

Waiting until she heard Sylvester call, 'Fiddler, play the Cotillion. Now watch me everyone. One skip, two skip, use the right hand to take your partner's hand . . . '

The fiddler started the music and Clare realised all eyes would be on the dance master and he would be engaged in showing the steps, so peeping cautiously around the door she looked anxiously for Captain Chatham.

But Peter wasn't there!

Clare felt the tears crawl down her cheeks.

But it had been her lot in life to overcome disasters. When her Papa had been killed and her Mama died soon after and she had lost her beloved home and pets, Clare had rallied and made the best of life. When she went to live with Aunt Maud and almost died of boredom, she survived, and now she would again. With a sigh Clare decided her best action now would be to return to Knowle Park.

Although very tired and aching from her fall out of the carriage, Clare quietly left the Dance Academy and made her way home. She chose the longer route as she dare not go down Hot Wells Lane alone.

How steep the hill to Clifton seemed.

*　*　*

Arriving at Knowle Park gate keeper's cottage, she felt she had almost no strength left to walk up the long driveway. She wanted to knock at the gate keeper's door and beg him for a drink of water, but she'd no time. She had to get back and tell someone about her ordeal and the capture of the girl at the docks.

Dragging her feet, Clare was almost collapsing as she turned the last bend in the driveway and saw a number of carriages parked outside the front door.

Had Aunt Maud organised a party and not told her?

Clare was in too weak a state to try and remember why so many carriages were parked outside the house.

Staggering into the side door entrance, she sat gasping for breath on the nearest chair she could find.

'Miss Fountain!' She heard the butler's voice.

Looking up she found him looking down his nose at her. He was inclined to be a bit stiff-necked. 'They've been looking for you everywhere, Miss. Lady Hadfield invited some friends in this evening to play cards. You'd better tell them you're back.'

'Yes,' Clare agreed feeling she hadn't

the power to get up on her feet and sore legs again.

Then she remembered Captain Chatham. How bravely he'd overcome his aching limbs and made himself walk again. So could she.

Stiffly, she rose and walked a little unsteadily towards the drawing-room where many voices could be heard. Ladies and gentlemen sat around card tables playing and chatting.

'Clare! Where on earth have you been?' Maud's voice rang out accusingly. 'And look at the state of you! I ask you, child, what have you been up to?'

Feeling dazed to be in a room full of people, and ashamed of her tousled hair, soiled gowns and dazed expression, Clare gasped to reply but little more than a squeak escaped her lips. What was worse, she found her legs were giving way and could no longer hold her up.

'My goodness, she's fainting!' Maud cried.

It was true. Clare could no longer

take the punishment her body was enduring and she felt herself sliding down towards the carpet.

But some strong arms were catching her, and a male voice sounded as well as Aunt Maud's shrill order, 'Take her to the breakfast parlour, Rupert, I've had my chaise-longue put in there.'

8

'Miss Fountain!' Clare opened her eyes then almost screamed. She was being lifted up by a man dressed in an officer's scarlet coat. And his moustache was huge.

Her panic quietened when it was Colonel Rufus's voice she recognised. She blinked, seeing his concerned face staring down at her. 'Miss Fountain, are you injured? Tell us what has happened to you.'

A jumble of thoughts crossed Clare's mind. She struggled to say, 'I am well, sir. I mean I'm not injured. But there's a girl down at the docks needing help, sir. You see, Mr Sylvester, no I mean, the hackney cabdriver . . . ' she began, trying to put her fears into words.

'Clare sounds delirious,' Aunt Maud stated. 'I do so hope she has not been drinking. Lay her on my chaise-longue, Rupert.'

Colonel Rufus, although thin, was strong. He carried Clare easily into the parlour and placed her gently on the chaise-longue, saying, 'I think we should get her a glass of water, m'dear. She's suffering from fatigue.'

Maud hurried to the bell-pull, and when a servant appeared water was ordered for Clare as she endeavoured to compose herself. 'I'm sorry, Aunt, I didn't know you had company but I must — '

'Don't concern yourself. Rupert isn't really company,' Maud stated, 'he's, well different from ordinary company . . . '

Rupert Rufus explained, 'Young lady, I think your aunt means to say, I have become a close friend and you need not be afraid to say what has happened to you in front of me. I am a man of the world and won't be shocked. Nor do I blab. You may trust me.'

Seeing that Maud did not attempt to

contradict what he said, Clare — sipping the water brought in for her — managed to relate the events of the evening.

'Well I never!' Maud exclaimed, with her hands conducting a dance in the air. 'What a lucky escape you had. But, but the other poor girl . . . what shall we do, Rupert?'

The Colonel was immediately in control. 'Now, Miss Fountain, I must first tell you that Captain Chatham was here at five o'clock looking to take you to your dance class, and we told him you'd already left.'

Clare breathed a sight of relief. So the Captain hadn't taken their disagreement seriously after all. It gave her a pleasant glow inside to think Peter had come for her and wasn't a vindictive man — not that she really thought he was.

'Where is Peter now . . . I mean, Captain Chatham?'

'We don't know,' Maud and colonel chorused.

The Colonel added, 'I could do with his help,' He strode around the room deep in thought. Then he stopped abruptly and faced the women. 'I think we should notify the port authorities and get a search for the girl underway as soon as possible.'

'So do I,' Maud agreed.

'And what about the dance master, Mr Sylvester?' Clare queried. 'I'm convinced now he was responsible for the attacks on women recently. He told me he was an actor and liked to dress up, so it wasn't difficult for him to impersonate you, sir.'

'The scoundrel!' the Colonel cried. 'I have every intention of capturing the blackguard and having him punished for his crimes, but we must first think of freeing the kidnapped girl. They can easily ship her off somewhere if they are holding her in the docks, or a wharf, or in one of the streets and alleys around the Backs. The place is full of seamen's boarding houses. King Street, Pipe Lane and Denmark Street are like rabbit warrens — '

'Oh!' Maud cried. 'How difficult it will be for you to find her!'

The Colonel went up to her and patted her on the shoulder. 'Don't concern yourself, Maud, m'dear. You will stay here and look after your friends and your niece. May I borrow a horse from your stable? I was a cavalry man. I can ride quickly down to the docks.'

Clare interrupted. 'But sir, I must go with you. How else will you know where the girl was taken and is now hidden?'

Colonel Rufus pulled at his moustache thoughtfully.

'Rupert, you shan't take Clare!' Maud protested. 'It's too dangerous. Besides, she's exhausted.'

Clare stood up. 'I am rested now, Aunt,' she said firmly. 'I must go. I would never forgive myself if that girl they took instead of me was ill-used.'

'No, I can't allow it,' Maud said. 'I'de never forgive myself if anything happened to you. Anyway, you may swoon again.'

'No, I won't!' Clare exclaimed, swinging her legs to the floor and standing up, horrified at the thought of being regarded as a feeble female, 'in fact, I'm quite recovered now.'

'You are to obey me!' Maud pronounced. 'Lie down again.'

Reluctantly Clare did.

'Maud, m'dear,' interposed the Colonel, 'only Miss Fountain knows where to go. There are so many quays and wharfs at the port, I'd be all night searching the area. Our best chance to save the girl is to go to where she was taken.'

They all glared at each other, each determined not to give way.

The impasse was broken by the sound of voices outside, and in a moment the door swung open and Captain Chatham burst in. His eyes sought Clare and as he found her reclining on her aunt's chaise-longue, his grim expression changed and he smiled. Then he bowed saying, 'Good evening, Lady Hadfield, I'm so glad to know your niece is safe.'

No-one could doubt he looked delighted to see Clare.

Clare, looking directly at the Captain, and thinking she loved him so much she couldn't believe she'd been so cross with him, answered quickly. 'I'm not harmed, but,' she added in an urgent voice, 'there's a girl been abducted down in the docks. They captured her in mistake for me. We must rescue her without delay.'

Peter looked puzzled until the Colonel quickly explained to the Captain what had occurred, and in hushed voices they began to plan what they should do.

Clare rose from the chaise-longue and joined them. 'Sir, you must allow me to accompany you. Only I know where the girl was captured.'

'No!' Maud shrieked. 'Clare can't go with you, Peter. It's too dangerous. From what she's told us about that dance master, I think it would be folly to let her go.'

Peter walked up to Maud and said softly, 'Don't think for a moment that I haven't Clare's safety in mind. Indeed I have. No harm shall come to Clare. She will remain in my carriage and stay out of danger.' He smiled to assure her.

Maud blinked rapidly as she said, 'Oh, very well if you insist on taking her. But you and Rupert are to take great care of Clare. I don't like the sound of those villains.' Maud rushed up to hold Rufus's arm. 'Promise me. I couldn't bear it if anything happened to any of you.'

Rufus patted her hand. 'Don't you worry, m'dear. The Captain and I have been in worse skirmishes in wartime. Rescuing one girl won't tax us too much.'

* * *

The Captain's carriage-horse was tired, having been driven around Bristol earlier, while Peter was searching for Clare, but it was a strong beast and

Peter let him pull the carriage at his own speed down into Bristol once more, while the Colonel rode one of Maud's horses.

'So much time has passed since the girl was abducted, I do hope we find her soon,' Clare said with a heavy heart for the fate of the girl, but feeling pleasantly secure being seated with Peter in the carriage.

'We should go straight to the Port Constable's office to report the matter,' Peter told her, 'but I think it is necessary to try and rescue the girl first.'

His mind was on the difficult task ahead. So it was not the time, or the place, for Clare to apologise for losing her temper annoying him by trying to probe into his personal affairs earlier in the day.

As they rode down the road from Clifton and approached Stony Hill, Clare cried. 'This is the way the hackney carriage went. Yes, I remember it was at this point I began to wonder where the hackney driver was taking me.'

Peter sat forward in his seat looking ahead.

Clare with her eyes straining to see in the failing daylight affirmed. 'Yes, and we went over this drawbridge I remember. And look to your right, there's the Seven Stars Inn, I know we went by it as by that time I was anxious to attract anyone's attention and get out of the hackney carriage.'

'Mmm!' Peter remarked. 'We are entering the sailor's area of town. Not a safe place for landlubbers, but being a Sea Captain, it holds no fears for me. You are to remain in my carriage when I get out, Clare.'

Clare required no urging to agree to that. The light was going fast now and the narrow smelly streets, sounds of dogs barking and shouts of drunken sailors singing coming from a nearby public house where a brawl was taking place. It was enough to make Clare uneasy. She had no desire to leave the carriage.

'There, sir,' she said pointing. 'I'm sure that's the yard the hackney coach went into,' Peter halted the carriage by the double gates which stood open. He called to the Colonel who was riding alongside. 'That's the place, Rupert. Tie up your horse and we'll go and investigate.'

With the urgency of the matter in hand, Captain Chatham's injured legs didn't appear to bother him. He clambered down from the carriage, put up the carriage hood to hide Clare, and said. 'Stay here, I'll be back very soon.'

Both men entered the yard cautiously, leaving Clare alone in the coach.

'I refuse to be frightened,' she told herself firmly, although she could hear her heart had stepped up to a faster beat. But it was not her own safety she feared it was primarily Peter's.

His legs were not fully mended and although he had a well-muscled figure, he wouldn't be able to withstand a swarthy sailor or a hefty porter attacking him. And Colonel Rufus might not be able to fight more than one adversary.

Tense, she desperately tried to think of something other than the difficulties Peter and the colonel must be facing inside the yard searching for the missing girl.

Suddenly running footsteps could be heard and a man appeared out of the yard. Seeing the carriage waiting outside, the man untied the horse and sprang up into the carriage and taking the reins, flicked them hard getting the unwilling horse to start moving quickly.

Clare should have jumped out of the carriage immediately, but she didn't realise it wasn't Peter or Colonel Rufus sitting in the driving seat until the carriage began moving off.

She flinched hearing Sylvester's mocking voice. 'Ah, Miss Fountain. I have you again. And you won't get away this time.'

His hateful threat and the reek of

stale tobacco on his clothes were enough to make Clare cower away from him.

His claw-like hand had grasped her wrist tightly and she knew he had every intention of abducting her as the horse moved off at a smart pace.

'Let me go, sir!' Clare begged, trying to release her wrist.

She could see his eyes glittering in the dim light. 'What? And let you go running off with tales about me to the Watch. Not likely!' He put down the reins and picking up the whip cruelly whipped the horse to go faster.

'Stop beating the Captain's horse, he is very tired!' Clare cried.

Ignoring her cries he still urged the animal to move faster but it couldn't canter. So he swore and picked up the reins again and the horse plodded on.

A spark of relief settled over Clare as she knew any delay would assist the men who would soon be looking for her. She said, 'Captain Chatham and Colonel Rufus will miss me.'

'So they might. But they won't find you.'

Clare refused to be defeated. She turned her head and whispered through gritted teeth. 'They will find us, you'll see, you brute.'

In the dark with scant street lighting, Clare knew there would be little chance of anyone about — other than a few tipsy sailors. In this district a woman's screams for help would be ignored.

Struggling to keep on top of her fear, she tried to think calmly. Peter and Colonel Rufus would soon discover she and the carriage were missing. They would search for her. So she thought her best chance of escaping from Sylvester was to keep her wits about her.

'Mr Sylvester,' she said endeavouring to sound reasonable. 'There's no need to grip my wrist so tightly — you're hurting me.'

'With all the trouble you've been causing me, my girl, you deserve to suffer.'

'I'm sure my aunt will agree to pay you for anything I've done — '

His horrid laugh made Clare cringe. He rasped. 'What you've done, Miss Fountain, is to end my games. I enjoyed dressing up and getting my way with any woman foolish enough to venture out alone.'

'But, servant girls have to go out alone at times. They had to go about their work. They have no choice.'

He gave a snigger. 'That's their bad luck then, ain't it? Like it's yours now, Miss Fountain. I'll keep you bound for a while until I can persuade some bosun to tuck you away in a slaver ship's locker and sell you to the highest bidder on some sunny island. The alternative is to end it all for you. So don't get frisky or I might do that.'

Incensed, Clare's mouth went dry as she realised there was no point in trying to reason with a madman. Her fright had now reached boiling point. What could she do to save herself from the dreadful fate he'd planned for her?

It didn't surprise her to find Sylvester was driving towards his dance school. Nor that he abandoned the carriage and ignoring her cries dragged her inside a back entrance.

He hauled her into his small dressing-room. The sour smell of stale tobacco and unwashed garments made her feel sick. He pushed her down on the floor.

Summoning courage Clare protested. 'Mr Sylvester, there is no need for you to be so rough.'

'Shut up,' Sylvester snarled. 'Be thankful I'm not going to throw you in the river.'

'They will catch you.'

'No, Miss Fountain, they won't. I've been abducting girls for years and no-one suspects the perfectly-behaved dance master. Except you, you nosey little madam.'

With brute force he held her down and bound her wrists. Then a dirty cloth was put over her mouth and nose, which immediately made her feel dizzy.

Clare sensed he was preparing to leave. With her head throbbing she was in no state to observe his frantic rushing about to pack bags, which he lugged out to the carriage.

Barely able to think, Clare's fuzzy brain was just able to reason out that Sylvester would want to take the carriage away from the Dance Academy. And some of his dressing-up clothes too. He would want to hide any sign of the masquerades he'd been using.

A little later she lost consciousness.

Coming-to, a headache made it difficult for Clare to think. Sylvester was not about and she thought he must have driven off and left her trussed up.

She noticed the candle he'd left burning, it was almost melted. Soon she'd be in utter darkness until that brute returned and then she dreaded to think what might happen to her.

She would try and get away. But how?

Her bounds were too tight, her body

tired from the exertion of the evening, and she was sure he'd drugged her as she was finding thinking terribly difficult.

9

Blast!' exclaimed the panting Colonel. 'Although we've caught two of the villains, I saw the third one get away.'

Captain Peter Chatham, who'd been occupied tying secure sailor's knots to bind the captives' arms and legs, got up from his knees groaning. 'Ouch! My legs are killing me! I must rest before I go hunting that other one.'

'Yer'll never find Mr Thwaite!' one of the captives spat out, squirming in his restraints on the floor of the warehouse.

Colonel Rufus stood tall, 'Don't be too sure about that, my man.'

The hollow laughter the captive gave was not pleasant. 'E's a slippery eel if ever there was one! Thwaite's as like to get you first.'

'Ignore their boasts, Rupert,' Peter said quietly, hobbling over to the Colonel's side. 'First, we must get the

poor lass they captured back home
safely. Then we'll go and get the port
authorities to deal with that scum.'

The young woman had been terrified. She sat propped up against the
warehouse wall like a big rag doll. As
the two gentlemen gently assisted her to
rise she fell against the Colonel crying,
'I only went out to go to the harbour to
get some fish for our supper. I never did
nothing wrong.'

The Colonel assured her that they
didn't think for a moment that she had.
'It has all been a mistake. Those men
held you thinking you were someone
else. We have them securely bound up
now. They will be taken to prison and
won't be able to harm you or any other
person. I shall assist you home. Tell me
where you live.'

Still complaining that she'd lost her
fish and she hadn't the money to get
more and her family would be annoyed
not to have their supper, the Captain
suggested, 'Rupert, you take the lass
down to the harbour and buy her some

more fish before you escort her home. Then go and report the matter to the authorities.'

The Colonel whispered to Peter, 'I will, if you would be so kind to pay for the fish.'

Peter obliged by taking out some coins and slipping them into the Colonel's worn pocket. 'There, now I'll drive Miss Fountain back to Knowle Park. Later we shall discuss what can be done to apprehend Mr Thwaite.'

Colonel Rufus agreed and taking the young woman's arm said, 'Take my arm, m'dear, and I will assist you down to the harbour to buy some more fish for your family. We will go out the back way as it will be nearer to where the fishing fleet tie up and I'm sure we'll find a boat that has some fish for sale even at this late hour.'

Peter was pleased to see the courteous way the colonel was treating the shocked young woman and was sure that by the time she arrived home with something for her family's meal she would have made a good recovery.

But it was another young female that concerned him. Clare was waiting outside in the carriage and needed taking home, too.

Before he left, Peter went over to the bound captives again. 'Abducting women is a serious crime,' he told them, 'expect the worst sentence from the magistrate. But if you are able to tell me where to find Mr Thwaite — as he is obviously your leader — you may be let off more lightly.'

The two prisoners muttered to each other. One piped up, 'Captain, we don't know where Mr Thwaite hangs out. 'E's never come here before with a girl. We don't know nothing about his plans. 'E was going to pay us, he said, for keeping her quiet until the baggage was shipped off somewhere.'

Captain Chatham did his best to hide his feeling of loathing for the pair of cowardly villains. He was anxious to be off and drive Clare home. 'I'll tell the Port Constable you are here and he'll have you taken to gaol until your trial.' After that pronouncement, Peter marched off as best he could with his aching limbs.

When he got outside the warehouse he looked around for his carriage. Puzzled he couldn't see it. He walked around the area looking for it. 'Strange!' he said to himself. 'Very strange.'

As he stood he wondered if Rupert had taken his carriage down to the harbour for the fish, but Rupert and the girl went out of the warehouse the other way.

Peter scratched his forehead for a moment or two. Then a worse possibility came to his mind. Perhaps Clare had become afraid waiting all alone in the dark and had driven the carriage back to Knowle Park. Clare was, after all, an enterprising young lady. She was, he felt sure, quite capable of driving his carriage.

But it did alarm him. He'd told her aunt that no harm would come to her and he realised now he'd been too optimistic. He'd been a fool, in fact. He dreaded to think what could have happened to her all alone in the carriage. What else could have happened to her? Where else could she have gone?

He waited to see if the carriage returned from the harbour, but after twenty minutes or so, there was no sign of it, so Peter decided he would have to trudge back to Knowle Park.

It was during his painful walk back towards Clifton that it occurred to him that nothing else mattered to him in his life more than the safety of Miss Clare Fountain. And it was not only because of his responsibility for her safety, but because he was struck by something far deeper. He realised he cared for her. He was genuinely fond of her.

Buoyed up with this glow of being in love, his steps became less painful.

His way took him past the Dance Academy and as he came near, to his amazement, he just glimpsed his carriage being driven off down the street.

Bombarded by the sudden realisation that Clare might just have called into the Dance Academy to explain why she wasn't at class that evening, he made his way towards the school.

'Blazes!' He'd just missed getting a lift back to Knowle Park.

Then a more sinister thought struck him. Clare, he remembered was suspicious, thinking it may be Mr Sylvester who'd been attacking women. Peter quickened his steps, afraid of what he might learn when he got to the Dance Academy.

After knocking on the front door and receiving no reply, Peter walked around the building and noticed a back door, which was also locked. There were no lights in the house.

Hearing the bells of St Augustine's Church clock strike eight, he wondered why, if the class was finished, Clare had bothered to call. No-one appeared to be in the house. But something urged

Peter to satisfy his curiosity about Mr Sylvester. As the man was out he would take a quick look around the place.

As a young midshipman he'd been obliged to climb the mast and therefore climbing up a tree and swinging over towards a window gave him little difficulty. Once in the house he found a candle and carefully crept about the dank and tobacco-stinking rooms looking for clues.

'You are an idiot!' he scolded himself as he looked around downstairs. 'Captain Peter Chatham, you are heading for gaol yourself breaking into a house like this!'

Did he hear a response? His hand wobbled and he almost dropped the candle.

'Help!'

Was it a voice, or was he imagining it? He swallowed. If Mr Sylvester did indeed apprehend young ladies perhaps he had one hidden in his house?

'Anyone there?' he called.

'Help!' He was sure he heard the

faint voice reply.

'Where are you?'

'In the dressing-room.'

There, as clear as a bell, he heard the female cry. Using his knowledge of where the dance hall was situated, Peter was soon able to find the room leading off it. He opened the door and there on the floor was a young lady bound.

'Peter! Help me, please.'

'Clare, what on earth are you doing here?' In a trice he was down on his knees, using his nimble sailor's fingers to untie the unprofessional knots that bound her.

She could only lay her head on his chest and sob. Her wits had left her as the drugs she'd inhaled prevented her from thinking straight.

'Clare, who bound you like this?'

'Sylvester. He's gone . . . '

'What has he done to you?'

'I was . . . I was . . . ' began Clare, but was unable to make any sense in her confusion.

Peter hugged her close. 'We must get

out of here before he returns.'

He couldn't carry the candle and assist Clare, so the candle had to be left on the table where he'd placed it when he came in. But he noticed an envelope on the table with the name Mr Sylvester Thwaite, written on it.

'Oh, no!' Peter exclaimed.

Clare was in no fit state to walk far, and Peter himself was on his last legs.

Only one solution came to mind. He lived not too far away. He could carry Clare there. She would be safe, as Mr Sylvester Thwaite would not know what had happened to Clare or where she'd gone.

At first, Peter's worry was whether he'd enough strength to support Clare — who seemed to be have been drugged — to his house before the dance master returned.

'Come along, Clare, lean on me.' He was panting, sweating, with the effort to walk himself and to assist Clare as well. 'It isn't very far to my house. You can rest there.'

'I will try, Peter, but my legs feel like jelly.'

'Mine are on fire,' Peter replied, trying to ignore the pain.

Slowly, painfully, they managed to get out of the room. Without the candle, Peter found it difficult to find the door. But it was locked.

'We'll have to get out of a window,' Peter said, 'I can unbolt the catch.'

The street lighting outside gave him just enough light to see what he was doing. With many groans and huffs of effort the two of them managed to open the window and ease themselves out on to a bush which caught and ripped their clothes.

'Oh, Peter,' cried the exhausted Clare, 'I don't think I can go any farther!'

Captain Chatham knew exactly how pained she felt, as he was suffering greatly, too. 'Clare, my dearest girl, we are both in pain but must make the effort to get to my house. Sylvester may return any minute and find us.'

At the mention of Sylvester, Clare shuddered. She allowed Peter to pull her on her feet again. Somehow she'd lost a shoe, but by clinging to him they hobbled down the street. Each step was agony but took them farther away from the villainous Sylvester Thwaite.

'At last, we've turned the corner of the street,' Peter said, sending up a prayer of thanks. Only he had spotted the lively walk of the dance master returning to his house to find it had been broken into and his captive gone.

With the last of his strength Peter half carried, half dragged Clare to his house. How they managed to climb the steps up to the house was little short of a miracle. Hammering on the front door brought Peter's manservant to open it.

'Captain, sir, you are in a state!' bulging eyed, Hawkins stated on seeing his master clinging on the railing for support. 'And, er, your lady has collapsed, sir.'

'Quite so,' Peter retorted dryly. 'You

must get the spare bed made up and assist the poor lady to lie on it.'

'Have we been in an accident, sir?'

Peter replied, 'You could say that, Hawkins. Now don't shine your candle in the poor girl's face. Put it down and carry her in,' he panted, 'because I can't. I'm all in.'

Hawkins grinned. 'I can see that, sir. Let me help you into the hall. Now sit down awhile and I'll get your lady-friend in.'

The mention of Miss Fountain as being his lady-friend rankled in his brain. He sensed Hawkins smelt a whiff of scandal, but Peter was too exhausted to inform his servant about the circumstances that had led them both to the sorry state they were in.

'Get the door closed,' he snapped, as soon as Hawkins had carried Clare inside and sat her on another chair beside the hall table.

Looking with amusement at his master and his lady, Hawkins chuckled. The captain was a man who loathed

women — or so he'd always understood. So why had he brought this
young lady home?

'Would you care for a brandy afore
you go to bed, Captain?'

'I would. And the lady needs a drink,
too. Do you have a chocolate drink for
her, as I don't think she should have
anything — '

'Yes, sir, I can see she needs a
nightcap, rather than anything more
intoxicating,' Hawkins grinned again.

'And don't expect us to show a leg
early tomorrow morning, will you?'

Hawkins grinned even more widely.
'No, Captain. I won't disturb you.'

★　★　★

At Knowle Park, Lady Hadfield heard
Colonel Rufus's stomach rumble and
remarked, 'I suppose you want your
dinner, Rupert. You can have it. I
couldn't eat a thing. All I can think
about is poor Clare. What has become
of her?'

Colonel Rufus was pleased to see Lady Maud Hadfield prancing about her large drawing-room.

Ever since he'd known the good woman, he'd encouraged her to get off her chaise-longue and exercise more, and now she was much more active — and her figure much improved. But he was worried about her niece as much as she was.

He said, 'Maud, m'dear, you have a worry to bear, I know. Your niece is a sensible young lady though and I'm sure she will have an explanation for her disappearance. As for Peter Chatham, why you couldn't meet a better fellow.'

'I know,' Maud said, taking out her lacy handkerchief and pressing it to her watery eyes.

'So, m'dear,' Rupert said, 'I really believe an army marches on its stomach, as our arch enemy Napoleon would say. We must fortify ourselves with a good meal before any action that needs to be taken.'

Maud looked at him sceptically.

'As I was down at the harbour earlier with the young woman buying fish, I bought some beautiful haddock for us. It won't take Cook a moment to prepare it. You squeeze a little lemon juice, then some salt and pepper on it, and there's a fine banquet of a meal which will sustain us all night. Because, I intend to stay up all night — if I may be permitted to stay here overnight — waiting for Clare to return?'

Haddock, being one of Maud's favourite dishes, made her mouth moist. 'Why yes, you are right, Rupert. Of course you may stay here all night. And we need our dinner, I mean it is suppertime now, isn't it? Ring the bell and ask for that fine fish you bought to be cooked immediately.'

'Actually, the Captain paid for it,' confessed Rupert after a servant had been called for and had set off to tell the cook to get the fish pan out.

'Ah,' Maud said. 'We will have to do something about your finances.'

'No, no,' Rupert said, 'I apologise for being penny-pinched.'

But Maud persisted. 'I will employ you. For two thousand pounds a year, to be my . . . let me see, my secretary? How does that sound to you?'

To Colonel Rupert Rufus's ears that sounded very good indeed. He knew it was a very generous sum, but he also knew Maud could well afford it.

'My dear, Maud, if I was not a great friend of yours I might be embarrassed to make such a deal.'

'Good,' Maud said, sitting down on her day couch, 'that's settled then. I will make the arrangement with my bank.'

'Not quite, m'dear.'

'How so?'

Rupert came up to the couch and knelt before her. 'I was hoping you would be my wife.'

Maud's hands flew in front of her face. Her eyes peeped out over the top of her fingers as if she hadn't been expecting the proposal sooner or later.

'Rupert,' she exclaimed, 'What a time to propose!'

He rose from his knees and sat down beside her taking her hand and patting it. 'Love,' he said, 'is like an enemy's attack, can come when you least expect it. And we are most fortunate, you and I, that no matter what our personal fortune — or lack of it — we are in love, am I not right?'

For the first time in her life Maud knew she was in love. 'But we can't announce it yet,' she said hurriedly. 'Not until Clare is found, and is safe.'

'I agree,' said the smiling colonel, bringing her hand up and tenderly kissing it.

10

Clare slept soundly. The unusual sound of traffic outside her bedchamber window awoke her. Normally she heard birds singing in the early morning in the grounds of Knowle Park.

But she wasn't at home she remembered. She sat up in bed, feeling every inch of her body protesting at the movement, and gave a little cry. Where was she?

Then all the events of yesterday came tumbling back into her mind. Being abducted, not once but twice, and escaping from the attempted kidnap twice, too.

Ah yes, she must be in the Captain's house. A rosy glow came over her cheeks as she recalled Society's strict rule about being unchaperoned — and she'd broken it!

A smart tap on the door was followed

by it opening, and a tray was to be seen with the aroma of heavenly smelling coffee assailing her nose. 'M'am,' a deferential male voice sounded, 'the Captain thought you might like a cup of coffee.'

Hurriedly Clare hid all but her face under the coverlet. 'Thank you,' she replied in a squeak.

The Captain's servant, Hawkins, entered and placed the cup on a small table by the side of her bed.

'Hurrum,' the man said, seeming as embarrassed as she was. 'The Captain asked me to tell you, if you would care to take a bath, Mrs Cornish will come up with the tub and hot water if you like me to send her?'

Clare couldn't think of anything nicer and said so.

* * *

Mrs Cornish was a very small woman who told her she was used to working for the Captain. With a great deal of splashing she washed Clare, and her long hair, with rose soap which she took out of a pretty floral box tried with pink cord, which made Clare think the Captain had probably bought it just for any ladies he had staying with him — or he might have sent his servant out to buy it especially for her.

Then with a flurry of soft towels dried and combed Clare's hair until the sheen gleamed, then she helped Clare to dress it.

'There now, Ma'am, you is as clean as a new pin.'

'Thank you, Mrs Cornish, I feel it.'

'Now, I have brushed down your outer garments and mended a small rip on one sleeve.'

'Thank you, Mrs Cornish, that is very kind of you.'

'But your stays and shift are being washed and as it is a sunny day they are out on Brandon Hill drying.'

Clare pictured the washerwomen's linen out to dry all over Brandon Hill, which was an ancient privilege of the local people. 'Oh, and when will they be ready to wear?' she asked anxiously.

'It always takes a few hours for clothes to dry, even on a windy day.'

'Yes, I suppose it does.'

'The Captain has given me this robe for you to wear.'

Clare took the silk robe she was given. It looked new and was certainly not female garb. 'The Captain said he was given it as a present by some relative and it's far too small for him, so it might fit you.'

Clare was beginning to be aware of the compromising situation she was in. Her clothes may be clean and in order, but her reputation was in shreds!

Dear me. She had spent the night in the Captain's house with no female companion and Aunt Maud would be furious and probably give her the sack. Soon all of Clifton and Bristol Society would hear of it and there would be whispering about her behind fans wherever she went.

But it was better than being a captive

of Sylvester Thwaite! Captain Peter Chatham had saved her from that fate.

Consequently it was no use being missish. She had to face up to being considered a fallen woman, even though she was not. 'Where is the Captain?' she asked tentatively.

'I believe he went out earlier.'

'What time is it now, Mrs Cornish?'

The little lady was busy folding up the damp bath towels. 'I think it's near twelve, Ma'am.'

'Midday!' Clare was shocked. 'I must get back to Knowle Park. My aunt will be wondering where I am.' But the little servant was already carrying the pile of towels down the stairs calling out, 'Breakfast is served in the diningroom, Ma'am.'

What was she to do? Securely tying the knot of the belt around the silk robe she'd been given to wear, Clare decided as the Captain was out she would fortify herself with something to eat. Then she could face the world's wrath.

Coming down the grand staircase

barefooted was difficult, especially as the robe was far too ample for her slender figure. But by clutching a handful of the slippery material she managed to hold on to the banister with one hand and to steady herself, and felt quite pleased to have made it to the last step without falling.

Leading from the hall, one door was open and she could just see silver serving dishes laid out on the dresser. Not having had her dinner yesterday, the sight of the warming dishes, hiding the breakfast food, made her mouth water.

She went straight in and lifted a lid to see a pile of hot scrambled eggs and some bacon curls, her favourite breakfast dish.

She was about to take a plate from the pile when she heard a rustle of paper and swinging around saw to her amazement the Captain leaning back on his chair reading a newspaper — with his crossed feet on the table!

She might have slipped out of the

room, except in her surprise she accidentally dropped the warming dish lid with a resounding clatter on the wooden floorboards.

'Oh!' she squeaked.

The Captain removed his feet from the table with a soft groan. 'Clare, forgive me. My legs are killing me this morning.'

'Don't stand up then,' Clare said looking at him sympathetically, 'I do understand, I feel as if I'd been rolled about the harbour like a barrel.'

His chuckle made her smile at him.

She said, 'Don't let me disturb you. I'll endeavour to get my breakfast without dropping any more dishes,' and swinging round with her back to him she began to help herself.

He chuckled again. Whatever had given him the idea he could never be at ease with women around? And, although his robe was much too big for her his sharp seaman's eyes could detect a shapely form underneath the silk material. It was a shame she had to go back to Knowle Park.

Suddenly shaken that he could be thinking these thoughts, he picked up the paper again and began reading it.

Clare enjoyed her breakfast, and when Mrs Cornish came in with a freshly-made pot of coffee, Clare poured a cup out for the Captain, without even asking him if he wanted it. He drank it, murmuring, 'Thank you.'

I expect he thought Mrs Cornish had given it to him, Clare thought.

He didn't. He was hiding behind the paper wondering what on earth he was going to say to her. He was glad she wasn't a fidgeting, tattling kind of woman. In fact, she was very like his deceased Mama, quiet, yet by no means a submissive lady.

'Peter,' she broke the silence, when he was at his wits end thinking what he was going to say, 'I want to thank you for saving me yesterday. It was very brave of you considering you were in pain.'

'You were very brave too.'

She gave a rueful little grin, thinking she'd never been so scared in her life and it had been pure luck that she'd got out of the trouble unharmed. 'Is the girl that they captured safe?'

'Colonel Rufus took her home.'

Clare breathed a sigh of relief. 'I'm glad about that. I felt guilty they'd captured her instead of me.'

Peter stretched forward and patted her hand with his long fingers. 'No, never blame yourself for what happened. It was unfortunate, but all is well now, Sylvester Thwaite, and his two accomplices, are in Bristol Gaol. Colonel Rufus dropped by to inform me this morning.'

Clare gave a thankful sigh.

Peter's eyes managed to catch hers. They looked at each other candidly, and both smiled. 'Colonel Rufus had some other news,' he said.

'Oh yes?'

The Captain gave a little cough trying to decide how to put the news. Then he decided it was only Clare he was telling it to, so he might as well just tell her straight. 'Your aunt, Lady Hadfield, and Colonel Rufus are engaged to be married.'

Clare's hands clapped together as her eyes lit with joyous tears, 'Why that is splendid. Splendid!'

'I think so, too,' the match-maker Peter said. 'I believe they are well suited — '

'Rupert has given Aunt Maud a new, exciting life.'

'Indeed he has.'

While they were rejoicing, a sharp tap on the door distracted them. His manservant was at the door.

'Yes, Hawkins?'

'A carriage has come from Knowle Park, Captain, to collect Miss Fountain.'

'Ah,' Peter Chatham said, disappointed to have his time with Clare cut short abruptly.

Clare rose. 'I'd better go and get dressed,' she said, her heart sinking. Now her enjoyment was over. She had to go back to be censured by her Aunt Maud and possibly expulsion from her only home and position as companion. The spectre of a poor house loomed as Clare realised her aunt would not give her a good reference after she'd stayed overnight in a man's residence.

Her clothes were laid out in the bedchamber ready for her to wear.

'I'm sure they are dry,' Mrs Cornish said, who'd come to help her dress. 'Anyhows, the day is warm and sunny so you've got no worries of catching a chill.'

No worries. If only that were true! Clare sighed.

To her surprise, Captain Peter Chatham was dressed up when she arrived downstairs to get in the carriage.

'Goodbye, sir,' she said.

He took her hand and led her to a quiet corner of the hall. 'Why Clare, you sound as if you wanted to bid me goodbye forever.'

'Oh, no.'

He scratched his eyebrow thoughtfully. 'Then, perhaps, you don't approve of me?'

Clare looked up at his worried eyes. 'Approve of you? Why of course I think you are a wonderful gentleman.'

'Wonderful enough to marry?'

Clare frowned. She didn't want to start that argument about marriage all over again. It would be better to avoid that subject. So she smiled at him. 'I think I'd better go before my aunt has the vapours. I mean, she may need her carriage if she is thinking of going out on this lovely summer day.'

He assisted her into Lady Hadfield's carriage and then went to his own which was waiting for him.

* * *

It seemed a short journey to Knowle Park in the carriage. Clare was trying to think what she would say to her aunt. How would she explain that she was half drugged and unable to get back to

172

Knowle Park last night? Could she, dare she, say Captain Chatham had no intention of taking advantage of her, for she knew he was a confirmed bachelor who disliked women, and nothing untoward happened between them. They were escaping from the criminal, Sylvester Thwaite. Peter, she could say quite honestly, was as exhausted as she was last night and unable to escort her home.

On arrival at the house, she found Peter had followed them. He got out of his carriage and escorted her into the drawing-room.

Clare shivered with apprehension. Lady Hadfield, wearing a becoming dark blue gown was standing at the long window having what seemed like an intimate conversation with Colonel Rufus. They were certainly amused about something and Clare hoped it was not at her expense.

'Ah, Clare, my dear,' Maud surprised her by sweeping forward and kissing her on both cheeks. 'You look a little pale, so I hope you are well?'

'Yes, indeed Aunt, thank you.'

'So now we are a merry crowd,' she said, going back to stand by Colonel Rufus.

Clare, thinking she was entirely wrapped up with her engagement to the Colonel, said politely, 'May I offer you my congratulations on your betrothal?'

Maud and Rupert looked at each other with adoring eyes and Clare was pleased for them.

'And how about you?' Maud asked her suddenly.

'Me?' Clare's face became enflamed. Surely her aunt didn't expect her to confess in front of everyone. 'May I see you alone?' she asked weakly.

Maud took a deep breath in, then breathed out. 'Of course. You men go and wait in the library if you please.' The Colonel and the Captain left the room.

'Now, my dear,' Maud said kindly, 'come and sit down and tell me all.'

Clare was so thankful her aunt wasn't

cross with her. She sat down rubbing her fingers together nervously. 'Aunt, I couldn't help being away last night — '

'Of course you couldn't.'

'I mean, I had to spend the night at Captain Chatham's house. I was too drugged to walk home, besides it was dangerous with Sylvester Thwaite about.'

Maud nodded. 'I do understand. Rupert explained everything to me. That horrid dance teacher is now in gaol.'

'But, but,' Clare said with her face afire, 'nothing happened between myself and the Captain.'

'I'm sure it didn't.'

Clare smiled. What a relief to know her aunt wasn't furious with her. Of course Maud knew the Captain well enough to realise he wasn't the type of man to compromise a girl.

'So,' Maud asked eagerly, 'didn't Peter say anything to you?'

Clare replied trying to think, 'He told me the villains were caught and in prison. I was glad about that. So will little Annie Willis be — that's Lady Brocklehurst's nursemaid — she'll be able to take the baby out in the mornings now without worrying — '

'What on earth are you talking about? I don't want to hear about that. I want to know ... wait a minute,' Maud got up and went to her writing desk. She sat and wrote a quick note, folded it and handed it to Clare saying, 'Tell Rupert to come back in here and give this note to the Captain. And mind you stay for his reply.'

Clare dutifully took the note into the library where she heard the two men laughing. 'My aunt would like to see you,' she told Rupert who bowed and left the room. Then she gave the note to Peter. He unfolded the paper, read it, and smiled broadly.

'Do you know what is in this note?' he asked.

'No, I didn't write it. My aunt is much more active these days and writes her own notes and letters.'

Peter placed the paper on a table and

said, 'My little messenger, come here.'

Clare came nearer. But he put out his hand to catch hers and drew her very near so she could smell his fresh linen and cologne. Somehow she didn't mind that he wanted to hug her close.

'Will you marry me?' he asked.

'But you don't believe in marriage.'

His light kisses on her hair and forehead were giving Clare intense pleasure. His lips searched for hers. 'I've changed my mind,' he whispered before kissing her again, 'And it isn't because your aunt told me in her note I was to ask you.'

'Oh, I'm so glad!' She giggled.

'You'll marry me then?'

She felt she'd been drugged again, her head felt so light and radiant with happiness. 'Of course, Peter. It is my dearest wish to be your wife.'